BLACK BEACON

A Christmas Ghost Story

STEVE GRIFFIN

Copyright Steve Griffin 2023

All rights reserved. No part of this publication may be reproduced, stored in a retrieval system, or transmitted in any form or by any means, electronic, mechanical, photocopying, recording or otherwise, without the written permission of the publisher.

by Steve Griffin

The Ghosts of Alice:
The Boy in the Burgundy Hood
The Girl in the Ivory Dress
Alice and the Devil

Standalone Novella:
The Man in the Woods

The Secret of the Tirthas (young adult):
The City of Light
The Book of Life
The Dreamer Falls
The Lady in the Moon Moth Mask
The Unknown Realms
Swift: The Story of a Witch *(prequel)*

The Tree

Theo

Theo sat in his Beetle, waiting for twilight so he could steal the tree.

Elbows on the large steering wheel, he watched the hills for labourers, perhaps a lone herdsman from Mr Wolfson's farm bringing the cattle home for the night over the Beacon, or a farmhand returning to Friston with his shoulder pack of tools.

There was no one. Just the light silvering on the horizon as darkness descended from the tallest parts of the sky.

It was cold. The warmth from the fan heater, never very effective, had dissipated within minutes of switching off the engine. Theo sat back and rubbed his hands on his nylon trousers then fished his tobacco tin out from his pocket. He found the papers on the dashboard, prised open the Old Holborn, and pinched a few moist strands from the tin. The tobacco smelt strong, sharp, almost vinegary. A smell he loved. Theo stretched the baccy along the paper, rolled and lifted it to his lips for licking. Pinched it over, sealed it.

The light from the struck match brightened the cabin, making Theo realise it was sufficiently dark to move ahead with his plan.

He opened the door and stepped out into the bitter December chill. He stuck his fag in his mouth and pulled his sheepskin coat tight around him, wrestling the large buttons into their infuriatingly tight holes. Then lifted the driver seat forward and took the handsaw out from the back.

One last check up the hillside, down along the track he'd come in on.

Not a living thing. No man, cow, nor sheep, not even a lonely gull adrift in the sky. He was alone.

The end of his fag blazed as he inhaled.

Theo blew smoke from the corner of his mouth as he turned and ambled towards the wood, clutching his saw.

*

When he entered the trees he wished he'd scouted for a good specimen in daylight.

The remaining brightness faded with every few steps, crowded out by the sturdy trunks of elms not yet touched by disease, by slender oaks and the black skeletal branches of birch, such a contrast to their peeling white bark. Theo knew the Forestry Commission managed this old pocket of wood, some of it ancient, some of it new plantation. He'd seen from the brow of the Beacon that part of the plantation had been cleared a few years ago and was now surging with new growth. That was where he was headed now.

But God, he thought, he never expected it to get this dark this quickly. The mist from his breath was scarcely visible, but he could feel the warm ghost of it round his cheeks. With a final deep draw to the back of his lungs, he flicked away the small ember of his rollie.

The snap of the undergrowth beneath his boots increased as the wood grew greyer, more gloomy. Theo felt a momentary despondency, such as he'd not felt in years. Why was he doing this? He heard a ringing sound in his ears, aggressive and high pitched, the old tinnitus coming back. Like a wasp.

He thought of Nat, the sweet way she smiled, with the lines at the corner of her mouth. The worry lines.

That was why. He was going to make her Christmas. This year, they were going to have a good one.

He would make sure of that.

*

Dark shapes all around. A fuzzy hint of light overhead, barely penetrating the forest floor, the spidery duff on which he stood.

But at least he'd found his tree.

Theo knelt and felt around the thin, rough twigs at the base of the pine. There wasn't much space to get the saw in, make a clean cut. But this was surely it, a six-footer he wouldn't struggle to get in the back of the car. Something that would bring the living room to life, standing proud in the bay window. He imagined it all aglow with fairy lights. Nat might even like to buy a few baubles, some gold and silver tinsel, too. He'd saved a couple of quid on the tree, they would have enough for a few cheap decorations. They'd always scrimped on a tree before. With just the two of them alone in Black Beacon it had seemed an unnecessary – and a pricey – extravagance. He was sure it would cheer her up. Nat needed cheering up.

'*Verdammt!*' he cried, as the saw jammed in the damp wood. With no one around, he surprised himself, slipping back into German. Except for the odd *scheisse*, he hadn't done that in years.

He set to again, elbow pistoning back and forth. Stopped, wiping away sweat. This was harder than he'd thought.

Another fevered saw, then he paused, hacking phlegm from the top of his lungs. There was some pain in there. Ach, the damned fags…

Something called out in the forest, pretty much in the dark now. It was a bird, he thought. Not a crow, not raw or harsh like that. A more whooping sound. He didn't know his birds.

More sawing. Feeling in amid the denser, higher branches with his free hand, he found the trunk. The thing was starting to yield, he could relieve the pressure on the blade by pushing hard. He did that. A few frenzied hacks later and he was through, there was a slow crack and the tree fell, softly rolling on its coat of needles across the ground.

Theo stood and wiped his brow with the sleeve of his padded coat. He stooped and lifted the tree up by the cut end. It was quite heavy, and he couldn't use both hands because of the saw. He let go, eased his fingers through the prickly branches to find a balance point. Then lifted it again, and looked around.

It was dark. Dark and cold.

He wished he'd brought his torch. But he knew his way back, so it wasn't essential. He started to walk, holding the tree away from the ground. He didn't want to lose any needles.

*

An owl *hoo-hooed* amid the dark blocks of trees. He was having increasing trouble avoiding stumbling into trunks. There was still a little light bringing out shadows, helping him avoid the worst collisions. And the bulk of the tree was slowing and steadying him, so if he did happen to hit or trip on something, it wasn't hard to correct himself.

But... he thought he should be out of the forest by now.

He was back in the deciduous area, traipsing through a leafy mulch instead of pine duff. But he had been expecting to see the break in the trees for a few minutes now and there was only... the darkness of more trees crowding in.

Theo didn't have a good sense of direction, not like a man was supposed to. Not that Nat's was any better, they used to joke that the pair of them could get lost between the pub and the car. Never drink and drive, Nat would say. Wouldn't dream of it, he'd reply, I finished my pint in the pub!

But now he was feeling it, that shadow of hopelessness that came from not knowing, not being sure of where he was going. It was bloody freezing out here, he didn't want to be out for much longer.

He came into a small grassy clearing and stopped. He hadn't been here before. He looked up at the sky, deep purple now, the evening star visible to his right. It came out over the Channel, didn't it? Which meant he should bear left. The track with the car was on the, what would it be? – the east side of the wood, away from the sea.

He turned to face the knot of trees and was about to take a step when something moved in the corner of his eye.

Theo stopped and looked around.

There was someone there. Someone standing in the trees to his right.

'Hello there, man!' he shouted. 'You!'

The figure, just a dark shape, remained still. He was a half a dozen or so yards back in the trees, facing Theo. A woodsman?

'Hello,' he called again. He took a step towards the man. 'I think I... I'm not sure where my car is...' He looked down, embarrassed by the tree in his hand. Would it be obvious what he'd been doing? If he was a forester, might he get fined for something like this?

But the man wasn't responding. Theo must be wrong. It was just another tree trunk, surely, perhaps snapped by lightning?

He had that feeling of deflation again, like he'd had upon entering the woods. What was he doing? A grown man, stealing a tree he could afford... Even though their finances were particularly squeezed at the moment, there were those much poorer than him. In McFadden's, the bakery where he worked, there was Jonesy for instance, with four young boys to feed on less than twenty quid a week. And Mary, with her husband on the permanent sick. How did they make ends meet?

What was the point of this?

Theo glanced at the tree, then back at the shape. The shape moved.

'Hey...' said Theo.

The man appeared to gesture with an arm. Then he turned and walked away, deeper into the woods.

'Aye, aye, aye,' Theo muttered. He felt strangely spooked. Maybe the man was mute or something, couldn't speak? Was he trying to show Theo the way?

Come on, he thought, feeling things, his brightness of spirit, draining away, as if into the damp ground. To follow, or not to follow?

He followed.

*

The next time he heard the owl, he knew he was properly lost.

He was bitterly cold and only able to make his way thanks to the welcome appearance of a half-moon, lending a faint glow to the sides of a few trunks and the occasional patch of exposed undergrowth.

His right arm was aching all along from carrying the tree. He would have got rid of it ages ago, but he was a stubborn bastard when he wanted to be and refused to allow this escapade to become a complete failure. The forest wasn't even that big! He would be out soon. He should never have followed that figure – if figure it was, and not some figment of his imagination. What was the chance of a man out in the woods at dusk? At this time of year…

Scheisse, he muttered, the German coming back thick and fast now. Nat would be back from her bus trip to the chemist's now, wondering why he wasn't home. What a mess up.

And then, a few trudging steps on, there was a sound behind him.

A crack, like a twig snapping.

Theo turned and stared into the gloom.

'Who's that?' he said. The trees were dense, only a smudge of grey here and there from the moon. It was brighter higher up in the canopy, but what good was that?

'Who is it?'

Silence. Theo squinted into the darkness of the wood. A total absence of light, of movement. But a presence still, filled with living creatures, silent birds, insects, the trees themselves. All quiet, but all happening, in the midst of night. And…

Something else?

He felt a sudden anger, intense, irrational. He would not be scared. He took a few more steps and then heard a different, unnatural noise. A distant burr.

The soft hum of a motor car.

Without glancing back, Theo hurried forward, catching his shoulder on a branch, and soon he could see a clear line of trunks against the silvery backdrop of a moonlit hillside. Moments later, he emerged on to the side of the 259. There were no cars now. He saw the grey band of the road, heading down to the dip where he'd turned right on to the track.

He would be back at the car in less than quarter of an hour.

What a night.

Nat

She hated being left alone like this.

Nat tugged the curtains closed, shutting out the sickly sheen of the moonlight on the downs. Where was he? Where was Theo?

She wrapped her cardy around her and, taking her mug of Ovaltine in both hands, went and sat down in the armchair. She leaned forward on her thighs, towards the three-bar fire.

Nat looked at the television set in the corner. Cost a fortune, what with its famous *electrobutton* tuning. Supposed to keep finding the best signal. Why did he spend their money on all the wrong things? She sniffed and sipped the Ovaltine. *Emmerdale Farm* would be on now, that would have taken her out of herself for a while. The electrobutton thingamajig might be reliable but as for the bloody tubes inside the damned thing…

Where was he?

There was nothing to do, nothing to think of. Her gaze flitted about the room, the ribbed orange curtains in the bay, the gold-painted nymph lamp, the china dogs on the mantelpiece, Amber…

Amber. Sitting there in her armchair. With her glassy-eyed blankness. Disdain. Why did they keep Amber?

Oh, Amber…

Nat stood up and her Ovaltine slopped. Oh no, not on the carpet… No. Not on the carpet. It had stayed within the rim. Just. Thank God.

She heard a noise outside.

Footsteps, a dull thumping on the paving. The paving built out around the sides of the house. Coming round from the back garden.

Was it Theo? Was he back?

But she hadn't heard the car in the drive. She felt her guts churn.

Who…?

And then there was the clicking at the door. The key in the lock.

It was him. Theo was back.

*

'Where have you been?' she said.

He was bedraggled, standing in his sheepskin coat. He smelt of fags and the cold wind, standing there in the hall.

'Got you something,' he said. He seemed a bit ragged, bewildered, at the door, but then a twinkle came to his eye. 'Something special.'

'What?' she was intrigued. 'You're wet,' she said.

'Got caught in a shower,' he said. 'Close your eyes.'

'No, Theo,' she said, but her mouth was struggling against the worry, her lips curling up at the edges.

'Close them.'

She rolled them first.

'Come on, then,' she said.

He turned back to the door which hadn't shut properly and pushed it open.

'Open,' he said.

'A Christmas tree!' she exclaimed.

He'd wedged it into a pot with stones. That explained why he'd gone round the back.

'Oh, Theo, it's perfect,' she said.

He bent and lifted it by the pot, carried it carefully from the hall into the living room.

'Be careful, the needles,' she said, but he was strong and capable and he got it to the bay with barely a touch of the walls or furniture. She could hear his lungs though, the wheeze of them.

'Where did you get it?' she said.

'In town.'

'Mason's?'

'Stanley's.'

She looked at the top, the three little black buds crowning the leader. 'We need a fairy,' she said.

'Or a star.'

'Or an angel. I could go into town and get one tomorrow,' she said. She needed things to do.

'Put the radio on,' he said.

She went over to the hi-fi and turned it on and that song came on, the Christmas one everyone loved.

'Turn it up,' he said.

She did.

'...we old 'uns are the best!' Theo sang loudly and grabbed her round the waist. He swung her about in front of the tree and she knew there was no point in resisting.

Didn't want to, anyway.

*

Later that night, in the dark, in bed, she woke needing to wee.

For a while, her consciousness slipped and turned, in slumber and out, odd images of a ship, a huge tanker, offshore, its foghorn blowing, and a bird, a white bird, no, a sparrow, flitting, something to do with gangsters, the cargo…

Her bladder nudging at her sleep, stopping the images for a moment, you need to get up, then the ship back again, gliding on the dark water, spume at the hull…

No, Nat, you need to wake up properly. Get up.

But she was so tired.

She shut off the bird on the headland, flying towards the ship. They disappeared from her memory and she opened her eyes. Moments later sound materialised, too.

Theo was snoring beside her. A whistle from his nostrils, and another from his chest. The room was deep gloom, but the curtains were faint grey from the moonlight.

Nat blinked. She wished they hadn't had those gins. It was the music, the dancing, followed by all those songs, the Christmas songs that were so good now. Ever since *Feliz Navidad* by that Puerto Rican chap. You couldn't help yourself. They somehow made Christmas, which had always been a hard time, better.

Always hard…

She wished she didn't have to get out of bed. It was so cold. She imagined the floorboards on her feet, the iciness of them. She did have her slippers down beside her, didn't she?

She had to go. She couldn't go back to sleep with a full bladder. Or, not back to sleep for good. It would be more of this disturbed, on-off stuff.

She lifted the covers and sat up. Felt around with her toes for her slippers. Yes, there was the fluffy edge. She pushed her feet in and stood up.

She felt a little wobbly as she headed through the half open door on to the landing. How many… only three gins. Or was it four? But she guessed they were all large ones. She didn't know, Theo had been pouring them in the kitchen, finishing off the tonic.

Down the dark corridor, feeling along the wall for the bathroom door. Her eyes adjusting. There was a little light from the door, perhaps the moonlight through the frosted window? A little light…

She pulled the cord and squinted at the shock of the brightness.

*

After she'd finished, she stood up at the sink to wash her hands with the lilac-coloured soap bar. Squidged it around in her hands under the cold tap. Looked at her face in the mirror and wondered, who was that behind her?

Theo

He woke because of the scream.

It felt like a stab in his guts. He sat up, coughing, bewildered and scared. Where was Nat? He turned on the bedside light. Just crumpled sheets beside him, the bedspread and blankets thrown back.

'Nat!' he shouted.

There was a noise, like furniture moving.

He was out of bed, hurrying through the door in his pyjamas. Switching on the landing light. The noise was the bathroom door. It stuck in its frame in the cold. Someone was trying to pull it open from the inside. Nat was in there. Stuck.

The noise the door made was ominous, structural. It reminded him of guns, in the mid-distance.

'Love?' he was there, pushing hard on the top part of the door, it opened easily.

At once, he could see she was a mess. She fell into his arms and he held her tight, putting his lips on her hair.

'No,' she said.

'Alright, alright,' he said. She was shuddering for her breath. 'Come with me, in the bedroom,' he said. Before she let him lead her away he extended his leg and pushed open the door with his toe, glanced around the empty bathroom. Then leaned her against the doorframe as he quickly turned off the tap, switched off the light.

'Come on, duck,' he said.

*

Later, when she had calmed down a little, he went down to the kitchen and poured some milk into a pan to make some Ovaltine. Struck a match and touched it to the ring. It was cold in the kitchen and he stared at the dark window, the ghostly reflection of the room, of himself, standing there in his pyjamas.

He cupped his hands over the warming milk. Bloody freezing, this kitchen.

He shut his eyes, felt like he was rocking inside. All the blood stirred up.

There was a bit of warmth, damp warmth, coming on to his fingers. Not nearly enough to thaw them out but…

He looked behind him.

There was the kitchen in the yellowish glare of the fluorescent strip. The red Formica table and wooden chairs, the salt and pepper cellars. The bottle of gin, half full, and the empty Schweppes tonic water beside it. Their drained tumblers.

He turned back, prised open the Ovaltine tin. Heaped a couple of spoonfuls into Nat's mug.

Who was the man in the wood today? Why didn't he help him? He had just stood there…

The milk hissed and steamed as he poured it over the lip of the pan into the mug. He battered the side of the mug with the spoon as he stirred it. Then took it up to Nat.

*

She was sitting with her knees up in bed, the pillows behind her. The bedside light was on and she was staring at him as he handed it to her.

'That'll warm you up.'

She said something quietly.

'What, duck?'

'…him,' she said.

'Say again?'

'It was him,' she said and glared.

'Who was it?' he sat down beside her, prising off his slippers.

'Soldier.'

Theo frowned. 'Have some of your drink,' he said. 'It'll help calm you down.'

'Don't need calming down.'

'Was there something at the window made you jump?'

'No.'

Theo took off his dressing gown, climbed into bed. Took a couple of gulps from the glass of water he kept on the side table.

'You never listen to me,' she said.

'What's all this about?' he said.

'It was him. The soldier,' she said, as evenly as she could manage. 'He was standing behind me, in the mirror.'

'Aye, aye, aye…' said Theo. He pushed up his pyjama sleeve and rubbed the tattoo of the angel nestled in the dark hair of his forearm. Then pushed it back down, seeing her watching him.

He knew she didn't like that tattoo.

The Broken Star

Nat

Next day, she decided she would get the 9.15 bus into town.

Just after nine, she left their home that stood alone up on the down. Black Beacon was a white, pebbled-dashed house, unlike the usual flintstone cottages of the downs. It was a 1930s anomaly, built by Farmer Wolfson for his workers. Mr Wolfson was fond of Theo – his *number one herdsman*, he'd always called him, Theo had worked for him on and off since he arrived in Eastbourne – so he'd agreed to sell Black Beacon to them when Theo left the farm for a new job in town. It was a great break for her and Theo, Mr Wolfson gave it to them for a good price. They would never have afforded the mortgage otherwise. But with Theo's improved wage at the bakery

– nearly eighteen pounds a week – plus a small inheritance from Theo's mother, they'd been able to put together the down payment.

And so, here they were. Alone on the downs, in the house that had been a dream.

Once.

Nat walked quickly up the gravel drive from the house to the main road. The bus stop was twenty yards up on the right. There was no layby, you had to stand up on the grass verge. Stand by a metal pole on the side of the road on the top of a bleak grass hill. And there she waited, shivering in her checked woollen coat, hoping it wouldn't rain.

She couldn't spend the day alone in the house. Not with Theo working at the bakery, not after last night.

A gull came towards her, adrift on a breeze. She couldn't see the sea from the top here, you'd have to go half a mile over the down to catch a glimpse of it. Past the dew pond she loved so much, the derelict barn. The wind blew, she watched the gull battle against it for a while until a sudden gust forced it earthwards. The gull was close to the ground before it recovered, began to lift again and was soon away, veering sideways then flying up high and small.

An image of the man in the mirror flashed in her mind. Standing behind her shoulder, his eyes like chipped ice, cheeks spattered with blood…

Oh thank God – the cream-coloured bus appeared in the distance, lumbering down the road.

What a relief.

She watched it anxiously, not thinking, not thinking, not thinking…

The bus stopped with a hiss in front of her, filling much of the road. The driver opened the doors and she stepped in and took a seat near the conductor. He was a young man, clearly suffering from a cold, and he sniffed loudly – quite rudely, in fact – and asked her where she was going. She told him at the same time handing him the pennies she'd counted earlier for the fare.

He handed her the ticket and she gripped the handrail hard as the bus lurched away.

*

In town, she detoured to the library where she picked up a couple of murder mysteries. She smiled at the young girl at the checkout counter, who was wearing a lilac sweater with a safety pin on her chest. The girl had short cropped brown hair and black eyeliner. She handed Nat the books and seemed on the verge of smiling back before she checked herself and glanced away.

'Thank you, love,' said Nat, pointedly, as she tucked the books into her shopping bag.

The girl looked at her, the silence hanging between them.

'Alright,' she said, finally.

Nat smiled. 'I like your hair,' she said. 'It suits you.'

The girl smiled and blushed. 'Thanks,' she said quietly.

As she went out into the cold, Nat wondered at the frustration, anger even, that made someone become one of these new punk rockers. Hadn't she herself been bored, endlessly bored – interrupted only by moments of fright, when her mother flew into one of her tempers – at home? Yes, she could see why the girl might want to make herself different. She wanted to stand out, to be noticed. Not just to be overlooked. In some ways, Nat admired it.

She headed next to Stanley's, seeking decorations for the tree. When she reached the department store, she stopped and looked at the Christmas display that filled the windows. They had recreated a family home, the mother holding up a festive red dress, two children kneeling to open presents, a third standing on a stool to reach up and decorate the tree. Behind a partition wall, a man Nat guessed to be the father was lifting a knee to slide on a black boot, the final stage of dressing himself up as Santa. There was a sack of wrapped presents with brightly coloured ribbons slouching against his chair.

It was a beautiful montage, a heart-warming scene that made her feel joyous and sad and… something else, guilty, shameful even – all at once. She stared at the children on the floor, at the boy with the book and the little girl with the pigtails who was unwrapping starry paper to reveal a doll's house. The girl was a darling cutie. A little doll…

Nat hurried into the store. She moved past the cosmetics counters, the young girls all dolled up to the nines, staring as Nat as she shuffled in between them. There were ladies' clothes then men's, and a toy area with displays of board games and annuals, cuddly toys, Meccano and other festive treats, all draped with tinsel and baubles. Music was playing everywhere, Judy Garland singing *Have Yourself a Merry Little Christmas*. From the wonderful *Meet Me in St Louis*.

She would try. Again. Theo had bought a tree and she would try once more this year. She was determined.

The decorations were past the games area. They had a tall, bushy tree, wrapped with red-and-white striped scarves, decorated with fairy lights, silvery baubles, and that spindly, cotton-wool stuff like candy floss… what was it called?

She looked around, noticed a rather squat, middle-aged lady in a purple frock catch her eye and look away, somewhat disdainfully.

Miserable cow, thought Nat. She was only a shop assistant, what made her think she was so superior?

She looked back at the tree. It was pretty. Nat gazed at it for a while, enraptured. They had never had trees as a girl, they were too much of an extravagance, but she remembered marvelling at them in shop windows, in other people's homes in Old Town. Walking home from school in the bitter cold with Miriam Bonnyface, gazing in at these safe, coal-lit havens, cluttered with cards and festive decorations. Her council home was never Christmassy, her mum was always foul-tempered, chiding her balding dad as he sat in his deep leather armchair, fingering his pipe with half-missing fingers, each taken off separately in carpentry accidents. No, home was never safe nor magical. They – she and her dad – were always walking on eggshells, tiptoeing around to avoid her mother's temper, a product of her mercurial East End Vaudeville father and abrasive Irish seamstress mother. It had taken the chemistry of Theo, his chivalry and kindness, to make Nat aware of how different a house could be. How comfortable, and replenishing. How it was all in the people. So obvious, she supposed. So true.

At the top of the tree was a dazzling star, fashioned from glass. It was magical, intricately cut, reflecting tinier stars of light within itself. Nat imagined it sitting on top of their tree. How bright and beautiful that would be. Without thinking, she reached up towards it, to touch it – and saw a shape, a dark figure, rise up on the far side of the tree, through the cloud of white-spun needles, as if coming up from kneeling. Obscured as the figure was by the smoky, cotton-wool fuzz, she was still seized by a death-like chill, cutting through her spine and paralysing her innards. She juddered, physically shook, and then saw a flashing object in front of her eyes, showering darts of light like a sparkler. There was a high, clinking sound and she spun away from the tree, a look of horror on her face.

'Oi, you'll have to pay for that!'

She turned to see the shop assistant coming towards her, pushing at the back of her perm as if to egg herself on.

'But… it was an accident!' exclaimed Nat. She glanced at the shattered glass on the tiled floor, then back at the tree. There was no one there, no movement at all. She scratched at her cheek.

'You break it, you pay for it, that's the store policy,' said the woman.

Nat felt a flash of anger. She was going to say something rude but caught her tongue.

'You look almost pleased,' she said. Her heart was still racing, like a horse bolting from panic.

'Madam, how I look has nothing to do with you,' said the woman.

Now she looked sour, thought Nat.

'Mr Stoke!'

Before Nat knew it, there was a man beside the woman, dressed in a neat pinstripe suit and fingering his grey moustache. Leave your hair alone, she wanted to tell them both.

He was talking about the store policy, apologising but making clear she would have to pay. Nat was feeling anxious, the shape behind the tree still flickering in her thoughts. She glanced back nervously, saw nothing there. Then looked at the man.

With his thin nose and little grey moustache, Mr Stoke reminded her of someone, she thought... No, not someone, something – one of those puppets on the new show she and Theo loved watching on Sundays, the Muppet Show. Statler, that was it, he looked like that old fuddy-duddy, Statler! Or was it Waldorf, who knew the difference? She might have laughed then, if the situation weren't so wretched.

'Alright, be gone with you,' she said, swallowing because her mouth was suddenly dry. 'I'll pay.'

She felt like some kind of prison inmate as they led her over to the till and she paid for the star, which was twice as expensive as she'd expected. She wondered if she'd have enough for dinner and the fare home.

'Why's it so much?' she said.

'Handmade in Oxford,' said the man. She saw his name on his pinned badge. The woman was Mrs Shelby.

'I was going to buy some other things here today, but I shan't now,' she said defiantly, as they stood like guardians over the shop till.

Neither of them replied. The man looked somewhat sheepish, the woman a mix of indignant and triumphant, as Nat turned to walk from the store with as much dignity as she could muster.

Theo

'You're looking a bit down, mate.'

Ray. He always hit the nail on the head.

Theo pulled the tray of macaroons from the industrial oven, loving that sweetish waft of almond. He gently pinched the edge of one.

'Another thirty seconds, I reckon,' said his colleague, his best friend of nineteen, more than that, twenty – no, twenty-one years. Ray Teal, wiry frame, narrow face, dark, Italian-looking hair. Not a drop of foreign blood in him, though. Born and bred just down the coast in Hastings. From his complexion, he and Theo could be brothers.

Theo slid the macaroons back in, wiping his brow. He took on enough heat in a day shift to keep him warm all night up on the downs. Sometimes. Or at least, not when the weather was this bitter. He wondered if it might snow for Christmas.

'Time for a break when they're done,' he said, righting his back. There was a dull ache above his hip, surely from carrying that bloody tree round and round in circles in the forest all night.

*

'So what's up?' said Ray, loading half a doughnut into his mouth as he spooned sugar into his tea. They were sitting in the McFadden's staff canteen, bare elbows on the blue Formica table. Two other bakers, Steve Barron and the newbie, Jeff Cooper, were halfway down the long table, chatting. Jeff was making himself a rollie after Theo had slid his tin down to him.

'Nothing,' said Theo.

'Come on,' said Ray, his lips creasing at the edges, winningly boyish. Like he was fourteen, not forty-four.

'Nat,' said Theo, begrudgingly.

'What's up with her?' said Ray.

Theo paused. 'Just… a mood.'

'You know how much I love Nat,' said Ray. 'But she does worry a lot. And you, my son, need a break.'

Theo shrugged.

'Come out with us after work,' said Ray. 'Come for one down the Crown.'

'Nat's expecting me back.'

'Give her a call. She won't mind.'

'She will.' After last night, he was thinking.

'Go on.'

*

When the shift finished, he went out the factory into the dark and crossed to the red phone box opposite. He dialled their number and waited as the ringtone burred.

'Hello, Eastbourne 2142.'

He shoved his 10p past the resistant spring, heard it clatter down the inside of the phone.

'Nat, it's me.'

'Where are you, love?'

'At work. Just finished. Ray's asked me to go with them for a drink down the Crown.'

'Oh.'

'Do you mind?'

'No, love.'

'You sure? After last night?'

'How long will you be?'

'Not long. Just one or two.'

'Come back soon.'

'I will.'

'I'll keep your dinner warm in the oven.'

'Thanks.'

'Be careful driving. Don't want the police to catch you. It's nearly Christmas, they'll be out in their droves…'

Nat

She minded, of course she minded, but how could she say no?

Nat sat in the kitchen, staring at the black window. She could feel pressure in her bladder but didn't want to go to the bathroom. Not after last night. She was going to have to, of course. But not now.

He shouldn't have even asked. It wasn't fair. And it wasn't like him.

Ray had asked him, Ray Teal… He should have known better, too.

What was she going to do now?

Dinner. She would cook dinner. She looked at the fridge in the corner, thought about the chops in there. She'd picked them up from the butcher after that incident in Stanley's with the dreadful woman. And man. Mrs Shelby and Mr Stoke. Sometimes she wished she did have an ounce or two of her mother's temper, at least she could have told them what she'd thought of them. And now here she was, back home with not a single thing to decorate the tree, not even a bauble. With her nerves back.

And she was alone. Alone in Black Beacon.

She hoped.

The thought of the soldier made her stand up at once, her hands brushing over her hips and down the tops of her thighs.

What if he…?

Focus. Dinner. The chops.

But she wasn't hungry now, not in the slightest.

What was that shadow behind the tree today, the sudden movement that made her knock the star off?

Her stomach spasmed, she raised the back of her hand to her mouth. Looked round at the kitchen, the red-topped table and chairs, the washing machine with its two lidded drums, the blue hose between them. The glasses in the cupboards above the sink, the back door with its frosted window, facing out on to darkness. Just a small, square room.

She left it, went into the hall, looked up the stairs and thought about the bathroom but then not thinking, not thinking, she headed into the lounge. Sat down on the grey foam-cushioned sofa – modern and comfy, bought from Stanley's, no less, two years ago – and stared at the dead TV. Thought about how it was Emmerdale Farm time. Again.

Bloody tubes. Or whatever it was.

She reached for her book, the latest Victoria Holt – and saw Amber in the armchair, gazing at her unflinchingly.

I don't like you.

Where did that thought come from? It was unbidden! She felt a loosening, as if things were rearranging themselves inside her, and not for the better.

How could she think that? She loved Amber. Her little baby Daisy's only ever doll…

She stood up abruptly, went over and picked up the flaxen haired doll in its gingham dress. Amber regarded her with bright, sky-blue eyes, with gaping pupils. Nat felt uncomfortable the longer she looked at them. She held the doll up against her chest, concealing the eyes. She stroked her back.

Poor Amber. Where had that horrible thought come from? If she couldn't trust herself not to have evil thoughts, who, what, could she trust? What a devastating idea, not to be able to trust yourself, your own errant mind…

Oh God, what an evening already. And she needed to go to the toilet.

When would Theo be back?

The Figure in the Road

Theo

'See those two birds in the corner – the one on the left, with the red hair? Giving you the eye, she is…'

'Huh!' Theo pushed Ray away from his ear.

The lights were bright in the Crown, the air fuggy with smoke, the beer going down nicely. Everyone was laughing, talking fast in loud voices so they could be heard over that spritely Anne Murray song, *Snowbird*, coming from the jukebox. Theo swigged his pint of Harp and looked at the two women in the corner, drinking red Dubonnet, or something similar. One was blonde; the other, the redhead, did hold his eye for a moment.

No good, love, he thought. Not interested. He looked back at Ray, wrinkled his nose slightly.

'Just because you're on a diet, doesn't mean you can't

look at the menu,' said Ray, nudging his friend's side with an elbow.

'Absolute piss,' said Tim Knotts, the shift manager from Blackburn with the greying mullet, cut short on top. He was grimacing too, but at his pint as he placed it back down on the table.

'Here we go…' Ray whispered.

'Nothing like the Pilsners they drink in your home country,' said Tim, nodding at Theo.

'Drink the Bass like everyone else if you don't like it,' said Steve Barron, at six-seven the tallest man in McFadden's and the tallest man Theo knew.

'Ever since he went to that Munich Beer Festival, he has to drink bloody lager,' said Ray.

'I drink it, too,' said Theo. He looked at Tim and added: 'And you're right…'

Tim nodded sharply at him. 'Couldn't go back to the ale after that. Even if this does taste like gnat's piss…'

There was a cackle of laughter and Morris Jones, Jonesy, banged his pint down a little too hard on the table in glee, slopping beer into the ashtray. Theo wasn't sure if he was laughing at Tim calling the beer *gnat's piss*, or laughing at something someone said further down the table.

'Mop that up, quick,' said Ray, grabbing a beermat to push the beer back from the edge where it was about to soak his lap.

'Theo...'

In the midst of the bonhomie and commotion, Theo looked round at the newbie, Jeff, who was puffing on another rollie made from Theo's Old Holborn. Fleetingly, he mused on the change to his name, his identity, the way they pronounced the *Th* soft over here, not like the hard Tee-o they called him back in Germany. The real way to say his name.

'How did you get to be here... in England?' Jeff spoke louder, and everyone stopped laughing and looked at him.

He was a gangly youth with white-blond hair cut shapelessly round the top of his head. Not long like the fashion. Very symmetrical features, he would be handsome if it wasn't for something about his attitude, an insolence that could be tiresome.

'You'll be lucky, son,' said Ray, sitting upright on the bench with his customary look of bemusement. 'More likely get blood out a stone.'

Jeff shook his head a little. 'Go on, I'd love to know,' he said. 'I'm fascinated by the war. My dad was with the Sappers in Burma.'

'Yeah, go on, Theo,' said Tim Knotts. 'I'd like to know the story, too.'

Theo shook his head.

'Please,' said Jeff.

Theo grimaced and licked his lips. 'Tell you what – if Tall Steve gets his round in, I'll do it,' he said.

When Steve sprang to his feet Theo regretted it at once.

'Haven't you got the gift then, Jeff?' said Ray. 'The gift of persuasion. He never talks about the war.'

'Don't mention the war!' declared Morris Jones, parroting Cleese in *Fawlty Towers*. No one laughed.

Ray glanced at Theo, a look of friendship. Theo knew he would shut them down for him if he needed him to. But Theo's regret passed swiftly, he was merry, the beer was doing him good, and he felt like talking. If Jeff wanted to hear it, then why not?

He rolled himself another fag as Steve carried back a tray of jugs of brown and golden beer. Then, after striking a match and lighting it, he began.

'Well,' he said, 'let me start by telling you, I was captured in a battle that we – the Jerrys, that is,' he added with a quick wink at Morris, 'won.'

'And another interesting thing, it started thirty-two years ago, pretty much to this day. I'd been conscripted January that year. So many men had been killed they ordered all seventeen-year-olds up to the front. My older brothers, Berne and Jürgen, had been fighting for years – before both being captured, thank God. Jürgen in North Africa, back in '42 at El Alamein, and Berne more recently, on the Russian front, somewhere deep in Bulgaria I think.

'So it was only me still fighting.'

'Still fighting the Führer's war…' said Jeff, with a soft whistle.

Theo glanced at him, took a puff on his fag before continuing: 'Things were getting desperate by that time. France had been lost but the generals weren't giving up. They were placing all their bets on our new piece of hardware – the Panzer Six.'

'The legendary Tiger,' said Jeff.

Theo nodded. 'The Allies, mainly the Americans, were coming through the Ardennes in Belgium. They reached a place called Sankht Vith – Saint Vith – where they were stopped by the Panzers.'

'Were you in one of them?' said Jeff, eyes wide. 'Were you in a Tiger?'

'No,' said Theo. 'Not me. I was just an ordinary private. I was stationed in France for the first year, on the firing range of one of the first V1 rockets. Bloody thing went up in the air and came straight back down and hit the launch site. Every man had to run for the shelters!

'Then I was at Caen…'

'One of the bloodiest battles of the war,' said Tall Steve, tugging his earring.

Theo nodded. He didn't talk about Caen. 'The Tigers were doing a good job at St Vith.'

'For you Krauts,' Jonesy chipped in, grinning.

Theo winced, turned it into a small smile. 'Yes,' he said. 'For us Krauts.' Out of the corner of his eye, he saw Ray raise an eyebrow. Decided to resume anyway.

'Towards the end of the day, we infantry had all been scattered about. We were working in small units, trying to take out machine gun and artillery posts. The sergeants, corporals, they were really having to think, because the radios were all playing up, they were useless. To many hills and trees.

'After moving through a small copse our unit came under fire from a squad of GIs. They had tommy guns and we took heavy casualties before a personnel carrier turned up and scattered them.

'One of our grenadiers was killed in the gunfight and the Sergeant, Hans Angert, told me to get his anti-tank gun.'

'Faust or Schreck?' said Jeff.

'You know your stuff,' said Theo, eyeing him. 'It was a Panzerschreck.'

'Did you know how to use it?'

'It was simple enough – easier than the Panzerfaust actually, although heavier and a lot more dangerous to shoot.'

'All that fire and smoke,' said Jeff.

'Yes. You really *do* know your stuff. And by then everything was so chaotic I didn't get any of the protective equipment – gas mask, gloves, poncho – that went with it. And worse than that, the guy who Angert told to help me, to load for me, was Dieter Anders – a real jerk.'

'Why?' said Tall Steve.

Theo went quiet, thinking, remembering Dieter, his height, the broad shoulders, a true Aryan with his light hair and narrow eyes. A man made for the uniform. And then he remembered Sophie Fischer, and the boy in the snow-filled alleyway…

'Theo?'

He looked up, saw all their eyes on him round the table. He coughed, then said: 'Why was he a jerk? Most of us were fed up with the bloody propaganda at that stage. Hitler was unhinged – *more* unhinged – and telling us, no, ordering us all to believe the war would still be won, despite no one having a bloody clue how.'

Tim Knotts snorted. 'Here, I order you all to believe in fairies,' he said and everyone chuckled.

'Precisely,' said Theo. 'But Dieter was one of those old school Nazis. He really did think we could still do it. I'd had a punch-up with him a few weeks before, after a drunken argument, something about the Herrenrasse…'

'The good old Master Race,' said Jeff.

'Yes. And as a result, Angert put me in solitary confinement for a couple of days.'

'Shoot,' said Jeff.

'Didn't know Theo had been in the old nick, did you?' said Ray.

'Course he did, he was a Prisoner of bloody War, you plonker!' said Tim and for some reason they all burst out laughing, even Theo. The drink.

'Anyway, things took a bad turn for us on the battlefield,' Theo resumed, after they'd all quietened down. 'A squad of Sherman tanks appeared with infantry support and we had to take cover sharpish.

'Dieter and I were on the outskirts of the village and we hid behind a concrete pipe. It wasn't perfect but it gave us a bit of cover. There was a tank coming towards us, a few hundred yards away from the rest, its commander sitting up on top. He was shouting into his radio, I could see him clearly, goggles up on his helmet.

'I was waiting for them to pass…'

'Thinner armour at the back,' said Jeff.

'Where on earth do you find all this out?' said Theo.

'Mainly from Dad, but I read up on it too. Books from the library…'

Theo took a sip of his pint then continued: 'So anyway, just as the tank was levelling with us, Dieter starts telling me to fire, as if he thinks I'm going to bottle it or something.

'I told him to belt up, but by then the tank commander had spotted us – possibly heard us arguing – and quick as lightning he swung the mounted machine gun our way…'

'Sheesh, what happened?' said Jeff, his jaw dropping.

'I realised I had to shoot straight away, and pulled the trigger,' said Theo. 'I hit, heard the clunk, but there was no explosion and the shell flew off and exploded in the trees.'

'You were right,' said Jeff.

'For all the good it did me. That was it, our one chance gone. I began to reach for my rifle as the tank commander sprayed us with bullets. The piping must have protected me, I didn't get hit – but I had a stick grenade on my backpack that did. It exploded.'

'Bloody Nora!' exclaimed Jeff. 'How did you survive that?'

Theo was swamped with a sudden feeling, like panic. He remembered the pain, not from the explosion, but from the healing afterwards. He… why did he tell this story?

But he realised he had to finish now.

He stubbed out his rollie on the ashtray. 'Somehow the pipe protected me from the worst of the blast,' he said. 'Still, I was ripped apart, scarred from throat to foot on this side…' he stroked his left ribs.

'But the Red Cross found me. Even though the Americans were losing the battle – or maybe because it wasn't clear at that stage – a couple of their guys came across me, I must have been semi-conscious, and they took me back to their lines. I was operated on, stitched up. The pain, it was…'

'And so you became a PoW,' said Tall Steve.

'Yes. Shipped to Canada, then Scotland, and finally down here, to our beloved hometown.'

'Where he and a young beauty named Nat Lycett fell head over heels in love,' said Ray, putting his arm around his shoulder. 'Every cloud…'

'Yes, every cloud,' Theo repeated. Then added: 'I met her when I was working on a farm up on the downs. She was on a day trip with one of her friends…'

'As if the Third Reich weren't enough, they have to come over here and steal our bloody women too…'

They all turned to look at the speaker, a stocky, middle-aged man, perched on a stool by the bar. He was wearing a heavy blue Fisherman's jumper with the sleeves pushed up showing a large silver watch on his wrist. Theo noticed how large and wide apart his eyes were, and thought for a moment of a picture he'd seen in a National Geographic magazine, of some barrel-headed fish from the deeps.

'It's a long time over,' said Ray, starting to stand up. 'Let me get you a drink, mate.'

'My dad and my wife's granddad died fighting you people,' said the man. He wiped his sleeve across his mouth. 'For our freedom. My uncle, he lost an arm in the Blitz. And now look at you there, sitting enjoying the fruits of their sacrifice in our pub.'

There were two younger guys with him, possibly his sons, thought Theo. He realised he should have gone home ages ago, Nat would be waiting for him, where had the time gone?

'Bloody Krauts,' said one of the younger men, whose face was badly scarred from acne.

'I was seventeen years old,' said Theo, feeling the nudge of something, anger.

Ray put his hand on his shoulder.

'Four years younger than my dad when he died off Gold beach,' said the man. 'When his landing craft hit a mine.'

'There was a big education programme, mate,' said Jeff. 'For all the PoWs over here. You heard him, the Third Reich virtually brainwashed them.'

'You don't go creating the deadliest war machine in history without the people's support,' said the man.

'Shit, what's your problem? Are you starting, mate?' It was Tim Knotts now, the manager, who should have known better. He stood up.

'Sit down,' said Ray, and looked at the man. 'Theo is our mate,' he said. 'He's been married to…'

But next thing the boy who hadn't said anything moved off his stool like lightning and clobbered Tim in the face with his pint. There was something almost comical in the way that The Brotherhood of Man's spritely Eurovision winner, *Save All Your Kisses For Me,* kicked off at the same time on the jukebox.

Before he knew it, Theo had barged the table out the way, sending the pints and ashtrays flying, and was shoving the lad back.

And then all hell broke loose.

Nat

She looked at her wristwatch. Twenty-past-nine. Where was he?

Drunk. With Ray Teal, down the Crown.

Nat stared again at her book, the pages lit by the soft light of the golden nymph lamp with its marigold shade. The heating was on but she still had to put a blanket over her legs to keep them from slowly turning into ice blocks. She could hear the wind outside, whining incessantly, intermittently whirring and rattling the windows in their worn-out frames. Nothing to stop or slow it on its journey over the tops of the downs, that was the trouble.

She wasn't taking anything in. Sometimes books could turn into nothing but black squiggles and marks on a page. She took off her reading glasses, looked around at the room, the Persian rug, the fireplace with its glowing bars, mantelpiece with its china dogs and carriage clock. The sideboard with the hifi on top.

Amber in her chair, cradled in the arms of the soldier in his grey uniform spattered horribly with blood…

She jolted upright, a sharp pain like a pick striking her chest.

Looked again and Amber was propped up on the burgundy cushion, all on her own.

She'd imagined it, just imagined it. Imagined him.

She jumped up, hyperventilating, heading for the kitchen.

When would Theo be back?

When was he back?

Theo

He had a cut on the top of his lip and a sore eye, but no one was badly hurt. Even Tim Knotts, who he'd thought would come off worst, had only been bruised by the blow from the pint glass, which luckily hadn't smashed. The barmaid, Tilda, had broken it up quickly, used to rowdiness from the big guy called Pete and his sons, Trevor and George.

They had all been turfed out into the damp cold night, Ray wiping away the blood on Theo's face with his hanky, advising him to tell Nat he'd had a fall.

'As if she'd believe that,' he said lightly.

'Try it,' Ray said.

Now here he was at the door of the Beetle, carefully feeling for the lock with the tip of the key, aware that last time he'd had a few he'd managed to scratch the paintwork. He couldn't believe the time, Nat would be furious. How many pints had he had? It was probably four. No, five. He'd be alright. He'd driven on much more. It had been a good night, except for that pillock and his lads.

Although he could see the pillock's point. He could always see their point.

The key went in and Theo thought about how his opinion of Jeff had changed. He was still a bit off, a bit too cocky, but he knew his stuff about the war. Especially about the Panzerschreck, that great lump of blazing, smoking, metal that at a hundred and fifty yards could immolate a tank and its trapped, helpless occupants. He felt sick to think of it.

He thumped down in the seat, pulled out the choke and turned the ignition. He smiled when the engine rattled into life then, just as he was pulling away remembered the lights, the number one giveaway of the driver who'd had one too many. He drove off slowly, staying under thirty-five in the busier parts of town, knowing there was a good chance of a panda car lurking around, especially at this time of year. The police had to get their own back somehow, with everyone else out enjoying themselves.

He slammed on the brake as a couple stepped on to the road in front of him. There was a squeal of rubber.

'Scheisse!' he exclaimed, then noticed the flashing orange lights of the zebra crossing.

The young man, arm wrapped around his wife or girlfriend's waist, stared at him in alarm.

Theo lifted his hand apologetically. He could have killed them.

Scheisse, scheisse, scheisse… shit. He was more half-cut than he realised. Perhaps the adrenaline of the fight had worn off. His hands were shaky.

Once the couple had passed, the woman giving a quick, unconfident look over her shoulder at him, he drove off, initially at a snail's pace. But he was soon out on the quieter, darker roads near the edge of town and he allowed himself to pick up speed again. The road zigzagged up through a patch of woodland and then he was out on the high road, no other cars around, an unobstructed view of the gold laced town below him, neatly edged by the deep velvet blackness of the sea.

Beautiful.

The town was beautiful. That was for sure. It looked like it had been decorated for Christmas, strung about with fairy lights. The human race could be incredible.

Theo took a left and headed even higher up on to the downs, Eastbourne appearing again then vanishing in his rear-view mirror. It wasn't long to Black Beacon now, just five minutes up the road, but he was dying for a fag. Sometimes, he couldn't wait.

He eased his foot off the accelerator, keeping an eye on the dashes in the middle of the road, and dug in his trouser pocket for his tin. There we go, easy, out and in his lap. Prise off the lid, index finger prodding about for the papers tucked away in there somewhere, amidst the baccy.

The wind buffeted the car and he leaned forward, putting his left elbow on the wheel to keep her steady. He found the Rizlas, could do this easily. Could do it in his sleep.

Slipped a paper from the pack, flicked it open. Then pinned it with his little finger as he detached a few threads of tobacco. There we go…

Now, both elbows on the wheel, fingers rolling the paper shut, evenly distributing the baccy, a quick check down, not enough light to see how he'd done, never mind.

He leaned forward to lick the paper, glanced back up at the road…

… and dropped the fag as his hands snatched at the wheel, just in time to swing the car left and avoid the tall figure standing in the road, right in front of the headlights.

The Beetle veered off the tarmac and lurched into the ditch at the side of the road.

Nat

In the end she settled in the kitchen, at the table, where the light, the fluorescent light, was brightest.

She sat drinking hot Ovaltine, trying not to look at the clock on the wall every thirty seconds. Closed her eyes, tried to empty her head of thoughts.

Not so easy. In her mind's eye she saw him in his grey uniform holding Amber lightly in his lap, holding her over his terrible injury, the horrific one she'd seen before – and she knew she hadn't imagined it. He had been there. What did he want, with his cruel, withering look? She glanced at the kitchen door, which she'd shut tight.

She knew what he wanted.

She hoped he wouldn't come in here, would stay out there in the living room or bathroom or wherever he was now. The kitchen was one of the few places in the house she'd never seen him.

Wretched, evil thing!

And speaking of wretched things, where in God's name was her good-for-nothing husband?

As soon as she had that thought she hated herself. Hated herself! Theo was not a no-good husband. He wasn't like that Harold Gibson, him who clapped his poor wife Biddy round the head like a child, even in public, she saw him do it once in the station forecourt. Or like Joel Davenport, who'd run off with that teenaged schoolgirl, leaving behind his wife and three kids.

No, not in the slightest, Theo was the man who'd saved her, saved her from the wretchedness of her own sorrowful life. With his smart brown eyes, his calmness, the pure, abundant care he'd shown her all these days. Something she'd never known before.

She remembered when she first saw him. It was summer of '46, early summer, June, she'd taken the bus up to Beachy Head with Miriam Bonnyface. They had gone for a walk up to the cliffs and admired the red-and-white striped lighthouse down below in the sea, then headed along the cliff edge toward the lighthouse it had replaced, Belle Tout, perched on a shoulder of land. That's when Miriam had spied them, the PoWs, at work repairing a flintstone wall. All in their pale blue shirts and braces, with baggy brown trousers. Nat had spotted Theo immediately, digging the ground with a spade, sleeves rolled up, tattoo showing on his forearm. She had a thing about tattoos, thought they were a bit common, but still, she was taken by his swarthy good looks. The others were all pale or mousy, handsome in their own way, but he was the one with the tan and the dark, curly hair, rising high and wavy from his forehead like some incendiary rock and roll piano player.

At once, she was enamoured.

Miriam saw the men were looking at them and suggested they cross the road and talk to them. Nat felt butterflies in her tummy, what an idea – but agreed. There was one there, Klaus, who was the talker. Pretty soon he'd got Miriam, up for it, all gay and bonny like her name, to agree to meet at *Rita's* tearoom in town. Nat kept quiet as the two bantered but noticed the way Theo was stood back looking at her, squinting because of the sun. When Klaus suggested Miriam came with her friend it was Theo he gestured to as the one who would accompany him. And so it happened, something utterly inconceivable to her only moments before, she was going to have a *date*… and not just a date with any old bloke, a date with a German!

It was too much, she felt sick thinking about her mum and dad, what they would say, but also sick with giddy excitement that made it even worse. When it hit home on the bus back to town she had to ask Miriam for a hanky because she thought she was going to throw up.

But she hadn't been sick. And she had, despite an anxiety that threatened to render her unable to walk, gone to meet Klaus, Miriam and Theo in *Rita's* later that week. She'd been so tongue-tied! She'd said water instead of waiter and called Theo Klaus by accident. When they'd come to pay, the Germans didn't have enough to pay for them all so they'd gone Dutch and she'd counted her money wrong, putting an extra two ha'pennies in. She'd felt so foolish! But all the time, Theo had smiled at her. When she thought about it after, she wondered if he'd thought her daft, not quite all there. She must have come across very young and inexperienced. Which she was.

But then, a week later, a message had come via Miriam, who'd seen Klaus again, that Theo would like to take her to the cinema. The cinema! She said yes before fear prevented her. Then changed her mind and said no, but Miriam wouldn't listen. So she'd ended up meeting him in front of the Cannon in town, panicking at the last minute when they'd realised that the film, *I'll Turn to You*, was about her idol Terry Randall returning home as a traumatised serviceman.

How gracefully Theo had handled it, suggesting with a wry grin that they go for a drink instead, which had cleared the awkwardness at once and made her relax. And the evening had been a swoon. They'd gone to the Dolphin, he'd bought her a half, which she drank slowly, while he had two pints and they'd talked easily about their upbringings, the things they used to eat before rationing, the games they played at home, his sounding much more fun than hers. He told her briefly about his capture in Belgium, then moved on to describing how the bears had woken him up at night in Canada by going through the bins. He avoided the tricky subjects with ease, a natural gentleman.

When he walked her home and left her at the door with a promise to take her to the next film that wasn't about the war, she knew things had changed.

Her life had changed. There was a big, wide open hope that life was not going to be so boring, so depressing, anymore.

Things were going to be different.

She couldn't wait.

*

Nat cried out, her reverie shattered by a shadow crossing the frosted window of the back door.

What was that? Had she imagined it?

There was a thumping on the concrete. Was it Theo, home at last – or was it that horrible spectre? Her heart felt weak, failing in her chest. She couldn't swallow. She looked to the door, shut firmly in its frame.

Who was it? She could cry with fear and frustration.

She sighed with relief at the soft grind of the key in the front door. She jumped up, opened the kitchen door to see him at the end of the hall, standing there in front of the night. He switched on the light and began to walk towards her.

'Oh God, Theo – what happened?' she said.

*

He had two cuts on his face, one on the lip and the other, much worse, on the top of his forehead. There were smears around the one below his hairline, as if he'd tried to dab the blood away with his handkerchief. She looked at it sideways and said:

'What a terrible lump! Come and sit down in the kitchen, I'll clean it up and put some iodine on. What happened?'

'Nothing,' he said. He walked unsteadily down the hall and she realised she would have to talk carefully to him. He was drunk and tired, and she didn't want him to lose his temper. It didn't happen often, but when it did…

When he was sat down, elbows on the table, rubbing his hands together, she asked him if he wanted a whisky. He nodded and she went in the dining room and poured a shot into a tumbler, brought it back through. He tipped it down his throat in one.

'Sorry, Nat,' he said then.

Even drunk, he was kind. Most the time.

'I was worried,' she said.

'I know. The night's all gone wrong.'

She got some cotton wool down from the cupboard, tore off a pad and wet it in the sink. Then leaned over him and dabbed at the caked blood. Kissed his forehead on the clean side.

'What happened, my darling?' she said.

'I drove into a ditch on the down,' he said.

'A ditch? How drunk are you?'

'Not... not too drunk,' he said.

She looked scared all of a sudden. Petrified.

'You didn't hit someone?'

'No... no.'

'Another car?'

He shook his head. 'Nah.'

'Why did it happen then?'

He scrunched up his face. 'Nat, love... I don't know. There was...'

'What?'

He looked at her and she felt a black hand pulling at her insides, squeezing her lungs. His eyes, they'd never looked like that before.

So full of weakness, so full of…

Horror.

He didn't need to tell her.

The Visitor

Theo

The next morning, he pulled back the curtains and groaned.

Outside, snow was falling from a dim grey sky, blustering across the sea-green down, settling in places. It was all he needed right now.

Theo eased on his sheepskin coat, feeling the ache of his ribs from the accident. His head was throbbing, a combination of the wound and the hangover. A quick glance in the bathroom mirror had confirmed his fears, he looked like he'd been dragged through a hedge backwards. Worse. Looked like he'd spent the night brawling. Which, of course, he had. The tinnitus was back, making him wonder whether he'd been boxed round the ears too. How was he going to explain it all to Farmer Wolfson?

The accident, of course. It was all the accident. At least he was pretty certain Wolfson would help him. Theo had worked for him after all, as a herder, merging his PoW work into his first job when he was freed and became a British citizen.

He opened the door and stepped out into the freezing, sludgy morn. It was going to be a long, hard trudge.

But at least there was one thing to be grateful for: no work today.

He tried — tried hard — not to think about the figure in the road.

*

Nearly two hours later, he was standing in the road in the stinging blizzard watching Mr Wolfson's Massey Ferguson pulling out the car and thinking, he couldn't remember ever having been so cold. Not even in that Ardennes' winter of '44, when at least he'd inherited a good quality greatcoat — an M36, he remembered — from the corpse of an officer who had been felled by machine gun fire. A few holes, but it was still enough to keep him alive in the freeze.

Wolfson's man, Harry Briggs, jumped down from the tractor and Theo set to helping him undo the chains, his gloveless fingers like a skeleton's, bloodless and ice-white. He didn't know how he managed it, but there was no way he would shirk this bit.

When they'd wrestled the chains off they checked the front of the car, surveying the damage. The fender was loose and there was a dent in the bodywork above the right wheel arch. A lot of soggy dirt and grass was trapped in between the arch and the tyre. Theo raked as much out as he could with his hands, then wiped the mud off his fingers with his hanky and squeezed them under his armpits to try and put some heat back into them. When he looked at them they were white and shaking and there was a sliver of torn skin on the back of his ring finger, oozing blood. Harry was back in the cab of the tractor, smoking and watching him, help with this part clearly being beyond a favour.

Theo smiled at him and opened the Beetle door. It jarred a little, implying some structural damage. He was nervous as he clambered behind the wheel, aware of money, their lack of it, and of the double hit if the engine failed to start and he couldn't get to work tomorrow. The consequences of losing the car – and possibly his wages – didn't bear thinking about. Why hadn't they thought ahead all those years ago and bought somewhere down in town? At least then he could have walked or taken a bus to work. Sure, Farmer Wolfson had offered them a good price, an unbeatable price, but they'd never considered the consequences of transport. Too taken with the austere beauty of the downs, that was their problem…

His fingers were so numb he could barely get the key in the ignition. He felt like his guts were rotting as he turned the key, his empty, beer-saturated stomach raw from lack of breakfast. He twisted the key through ninety degrees.

And sighed with relief when the engine turned over.

It cut out then, but that was normal. He turned the ignition again and it burst into life, flabby and loud for a few seconds in the boot where the engine was, then stalling once more.

Theo looked up at Harry, who was watching him bemusedly.

The third attempt it started again and this time, with a burst of revs at the right moment, the engine stayed ticking over. Theo knew he had to drive, and drive now, if he wanted to keep her running.

Moving her slowly forward, he opened his window a crack and shouted:

'Thanks Harry – I owe you one!'

'Lay off the booze, next time!' Harry replied, with a grin. His hair was shaved close like one of those young skinheads, but he had to be fifty if he was a day.

It was that obvious, Theo thought, as he turned on the wipers to clear the sludge.

Except, of course, the booze wasn't the reason.

*

By rights, he should have driven straight home.

But instead he had swung the car back around and headed downhill, towards Eastbourne. There was something he needed to do.

The town came into view as he swung right at the T-junction, the sea a grim, grinding green, trailed with thin waves of grey spume. It made him shudder with cold, just seeing it.

Soon after, he was down in the conurbation, the Beetle's engine making a low knocking sound alongside its normal responsive throb. Snow splatted the windscreen before being swept aside by the clumpy wipers. People marched around in trench coats, stooped under black brollies. Shop lights showed Santas and fairy lights and tinsel. With the heavy cloud and snow, the day seemed barely to have taken hold. He wished his head didn't hurt so much.

Theo found a parking spot a hundred yards down from his destination, swung the VW in smoothly and then, with a moment of trepidation – would she start again? – killed the engine.

He climbed out, locked her up, and walked down the street. When he reached the department store, Stanley's, he paused, gazing at the family Christmas display. The dad dressed as Father Christmas. The mum holding up her pretty frock. The little boy and girl on their knees, excitedly digging at presents, the other boy on a stool, decorating the tree.

A different life…

Theo grimaced, turned, and sauntered into the store.

*

When he saw the Christmas section, just past the games area, he paused again, looking around for the till. Almost at once he started, as a woman appeared from nowhere, sweeping past him with a cursory glance. *Mrs Shelby, Shop Floor Assistant*, her badge read. He looked disinterestedly at the packs of Christmas cards as she resumed her position behind the till.

That was going to make things difficult…

He drifted back into Menswear, looking at the cotton shirts. There was a good quality red-and-green plaid one that took his fancy. But at two pounds, he'd give it a miss. Perhaps a present, it would look nice for Christmas? He'd mention it to Nat, in case she hadn't got him anything yet. She still had tomorrow.

A young lady came past him, pulling a tartan trolley. She wore a long raincoat and a pink headscarf covered her hair. Red, horn-rimmed spectacles. Theo watched from the corner of his eye as she appraised a can of snow spray and a couple of packs of tinsel, then made her decision and took them to the till.

Now was his moment.

He pulled the plastic Co-op bag out of his pocket and went to the bauble section. With a quick glance at Mrs Shelby – the awful snoot Nat had told him about, now talking obsequiously to the woman – he reached out and crammed a box of baubles into the bag, quickly adding a pack of fairy lights and a gold star for luck. He turned and began to march out of the store.

'Excuse me, sir…'

He jumped, his heart accelerating as he glanced behind him. A tall man in a suit was approaching.

'Yes?' he said, feeling sweat prickle on his head.

'What have you got in that bag?'

Theo glanced down. 'Shopping,' he said.

'Can I see?' It was Mr Stoke, his name was on his badge. Nat had told Theo about him, too. They had both talked down to her, like she was no good. That's what she'd told him late last night, after they'd had a drink and calmed down.

He began to lift the bag, was even in the process of opening it, when he realised how stupid that would be. He would end up in a cell, locked up for Christmas!

Fleetingly, he remembered another cell, cold and damp, in a terrible winter, a winter of howling winds and grinding despair. A beetle, black, no, a cockroach, on the wall, its antennae feeling the air by his cheek, a rumbling outside, the sound of a tank, or a people carrier, whistling and rumbling…

'No…' he muttered, feeling dizzy.

He ran.

Nat

She was pulling out sheets from the Hotpoint toploader when someone knocked on the door.

She turned and walked out of the kitchen and into the hall. Cocking her head to one side, she could see a shape shuffling about in the vertical, frosted glass panel in the front door. She wasn't nervous, she knew who it was this time. In fact, she was the opposite. Excited.

'Hello!' The woman on the other side of the door wasn't who she was expecting. She was tall, with a neat black hat and a long coat that looked to be made of a fine, worsted wool. Her auburn hair fanned in neat waves from around her hat. Her mouth was very red, painted with lipstick. She said something else, in the cold morning air.

'Oh...' said Nat.

'Well, aren't you going to give me a hug?' said the woman, and said something else again. It made Nat confused.

As the tall woman opened her arms Nat opened hers too. Tentatively, they embraced. Nat had the impression of being watched. Was there someone up the hill, in the snow, a figure...?

'Can I come in?'

'Oh,' said Nat again. 'Yes – yes. I thought...'

The young woman was such a bright presence in their dull, dowdy hall. She stood on their ochre carpet and looked around expectantly. There was a painting of Geronimo on the wall, almost abstract, the Chief's face in yellow, orange and red against a black backdrop. Nat wondered about it. Would she like it? Nat had inherited it from her own mother.

After a pause – a long pause – Nat realised she was supposed to say or do something. The woman was gazing at her. Her eyes were shining.

'Would you like some tea?' said Nat.

'Thanks,' said the woman and used the word again, the word that so confused Nat. 'Shall I go in here?' She gestured at the living room door, ajar.

Nat nodded.

The woman began to enter the room, then turned and looked over her shoulder at Nat. 'I'm really looking forward to catching up,' she said.

*

In the kitchen, Nat worried about the tea. Did she like it strong? How many sugars? She knew she should know this. She decided to make a pot with a milk jug, that would show she hadn't forgotten.

Forgotten?

She was so confused. She felt sad and worried and excited and happy all at once. She hoped she wasn't going to cry.

Again.

Theo

Even with the hangover and splitting headache, he was fast.

Theo easily outran Mr Stoke and shoved aside a man he assumed to be a plain clothes security guard, who tried to tackle him as he was fleeing from the store. The latter came out after him on to the high street and Theo continued running through the sleet and snow, swerving to avoid people and their umbrellas. He hoped no one would recognise him, thought it unlikely…

With the man still behind him, shouting, he realised he couldn't go back to the car. A young man in green overalls stepped away and looked down as he skidded past. An old lady, small and shrewish and blue-haired, yelled at him to slow down but he ignored her.

He took a sharp left down a side lane, ran fast, took a right, realised after another hundred yards that the man was no longer following him.

He stopped and clutched his knees, gasping for breath. The bag, in his left hand, touched down into a slushy puddle. His lungs were aching, there was a pain like a twinging nerve right down the centre of his forehead. But he had got away.

And he had shown those pompous little jobsworths what for. If they were going to insult his wife, make her pay for their broken star, he had at least got his own back on them.

But… what a silly thing to do. A petty thing. Like stealing the tree. What had got into him these last few days?

'Aye, aye, aye, aye, aye…' he muttered, straightening up. 'What a bloody fool you are, Theo Webber.'

It was then that he saw him.

He was standing towards the end of the alley, beside some overflowing restaurant dustbins. He was tall and his back was straight, showing off to full effect his pristine uniform.

Theo gazed in awe at the peaked cap, the pressed, field-grey viscose tunic, those jackboots…

And then thought, what's he doing here, in Eastbourne?

Nat

'So how have you been?' said the fresh-faced young woman.

After a beat she added the unfamiliar word and Nat felt embarrassed as the cup she was passing to her tinkled in its saucer. She hoped it wouldn't spill as she set it down carefully in front of her.

'Fine,' she said, then added: 'Theo put the car in a ditch on his way home last night.' She wondered if she should call him something else.

'Oh no,' said the woman, smiling and raising a hand to her red lips. 'He's alright, I hope?'

Nat nodded, noticing how the women's lower teeth were a little uneven. The only thing about her that might not be considered perfect. 'He had a bit of a knock on the head,' she said. 'Some bruises.'

The woman asked something, said another incomprehensibly strange word. Nat stared at her, at her bright, crystal green eyes. She wondered why she hadn't taken off her coat and hat. The central heating was on. Wasn't it warm enough for her? The hat looked old-fashioned, a little black continental bonnet.

The woman spoke again. One word. Baffling. Querying.

A moment passed. Nat realised she was staring at the woman, open mouthed.

'Oh, he's gone to Mr Wolfson's farm to see if he will go and pull the car out with his tractor.'

'He's gone into town.'

The woman seemed so certain. 'No, he's just collecting the tractor,' said Nat. 'Sorry, collecting the car.' She laughed and the woman laughed too and she felt herself relax again. She always mixed up her words when she was…

Happy. She was happy. Should be happy.

Why wasn't the girl drinking her tea? Had she left it too long, was it stewed?

'Would you like a biscuit?' she said, gesturing to the small plate of pink Rivington wafers and chocolate Bourbons.

The woman shook her head. Her auburn hair shivered against the collar of her coat.

'It's lovely to see you,' said Nat.

'We should do this more often,' said the woman.

'I'd like that,' said Nat. She felt something inside her chest, an unusual emotion. Like her heart could break, burst open with joy.

'...see things more clearly now,' said the woman.

She looked significantly at Nat. She worried that she'd missed the start of what the woman had said.

'More clearly?' she said.

'Yes,' said the woman. 'Sometimes the shock of a knock – well, it can shake things up. It might be for the better, help him to see things more clearly. Important things.'

'Oh yes,' said Nat, pretending to understand. 'I expect you're right...' She paused, then added tentatively, oh so quietly: 'Love.'

She was rewarded with the brightest smile. Despite their crookedness, the woman's teeth were white, well cared for, and she had wonderful lips. Like a film star. Nat felt proud.

'Well, I guess I must be going.'

Nat felt a constriction in her chest. 'No...' she said. 'The weather... it's so cold...'

The woman smiled, but without opening her mouth. 'I'll be fine,' she said.

'Are you... walking?'

The girl nodded. 'I'll be fine,' she repeated. 'My friend has gone into town. But he will be coming back for me.'

'Friend?'

'Yes. Up the hill.'

Nat frowned. She remembered the figure in the distance, up the hill, when she'd opened the front door. 'Are you sure, that coat, it's...' But it did look well-made. Woollen. Black. Not the style these days. Nat wondered where she'd bought it from.

'You worry too much,' said the woman, before adding the word that baffled Nat so. She stood, surmised the meagre living room, the useless TV set, the embarrassing lamp, the china dogs, rug...

When her eyes fell on Amber she stopped. Nat felt as if her heart had dropped through the soles of her feet. When it returned to her chest it was bouncing about like a scared rabbit.

The girl walked over to the doll on the armchair. She reached down and seemed to cradle its blonde locks. Then she turned and looked at Nat.

'You look like you've seen a ghost,' she said, smiling.

Theo

He'd been following him for a while now.

As soon as he'd seen him there, in his uniform in the alleyway, Theo felt like he'd taken a very simple little step, so easy to take, out of this world and into the old one. He was back in Caen, moving down streets where the natives kept their heads down and shifted aside, attempting invisibility in his presence, in the presence of the entitled creature that he was. In the presence of him and his kind, the alien occupiers.

Where was the soldier going? For a moment, he thought he'd lost him amid the umbrellas, the giant, awkward black domes obstructing the pavement. Theo surged forward, still clutching the Co-op bag with the baubles in his cold fingers. He barged past a man whose expression turned from anger to apology when he saw Theo's face.

As it should be. Know your place. But he couldn't help notice the hint of insolence, the resentment.

Theo caught sight of the man again, up ahead, a white face with a pinkish hue, gazing at him as he crossed the busy road. Theo knew he had to catch up with him. There were staff cars trundling past, big black wheel arches, shining fenders, a rumbling he guessed was the tanks coming, hopefully those Panzer VIs, the fearsome Tigers. That would keep them safe. That's all they wanted now, to be safe. But such a long way down the line now, victory, as they were, let's face it, overall... they were in retreat. The Third Reich, the greatest fighting force the world had ever seen. In retreat.

A horn blared as he jumped out into the traffic, following the *Obersoldat* who was disappearing down a side street. Theo barely noticed the car that stopped, checked quickly to make sure he wasn't about to be pulverised by something coming down the far side of the road, then raced across to the side street.

There was no one there, it was just a small connecting passage between two thoroughfares. Theo walked down it slowly, in the centre of the road, feeling the sleet on his head, his hair soaking through, no longer providing any protection from the cold wet.

Where had he gone?

Theo peered into the two, three doorways he passed, but saw nothing. The soldier had disappeared. Something prickled down his spine and once again he was in another time, another town, small dark crosses buzzing high overhead and bombs thundering, a panic that scratched at your throat, life an ever-present trap about to be sprung, and now green uniforms were appearing at the end of the street, he needed to hide, leapt into one of those doorways, the door was open but even as he yanked the handle he heard a cry and saw from the corner of his eye one of the soldiers was running after him, he was sure they had one of those British machine guns with the loader that stuck out the side, a Sten gun, *scheisse*, the room beyond was little more than a bloody store cupboard, there was nowhere for him to go and he was out of ammo and *scheisse*, the door was opening again behind him, he had to take cover as he saw the machine gunner, he pressed himself face first into the wall behind a metal shelf filled with boxes and then *thump-thump-thump-thump-thump*, the bullets were flying, was he far enough in, was his back hit? Was he alive even, in the midst of all this shock and terror?

He stopped, here, now, in this street, in Eastbourne, his breath a twisting, ragged thorn in his chest.

He never knew how he'd survived in that small room in Caen. But when he'd finally eased himself away from the wall, looked back over his shoulder, there was no sign of that soldier. Just, for a beat, silence. Swiftly replaced by the boom of guns, the plunging of bombs, the senseless destruction of architecture, and the lives that shaped and were shaped by it.

Theo wiped his forehead with his sleeve. He was hot, prickling with sweat, despite the freezing cold.

He decided he would walk to the end of the street. Then, if he didn't see the soldier, he was going back to his car, going home. He needed his wife, his wonderful wife. He needed Nat.

But when he got to the end of the street and looked down the next, he saw him again, fifty yards away. He was standing still, gazing up at a house, a 1930s redbrick semi, built a little above street level. Built on the humble start of a hill, the very lip of the downs, the Sussex downs. A privet hedge, still green, delineated the small front garden set back from the street.

Theo tried to swallow but couldn't.

He knew that house. He knew it well.

Nat

She jumped out of her skin when someone banged on the door again.

Nat had been sitting at the kitchen table simply… doing nothing. Staring. Almost like she was shut down, like a machine, like one of those robots on *Tomorrow's World*. Without any batteries, power.

Was it *her*, the woman, back again? She felt a gnawing

in her gut, nerves. Maybe she should go to the doctor, get some pills, maybe something that could stop her seeing the soldier…

She stood and looked down the hall. There was a shape in the vertical pane again. It reached forward and there was a *rat-a-tat-tat* of the knocker.

'I'm coming,' she said.

When she opened the door her eyes widened with surprise. 'Tina!'

'Hello, Nat,' said the woman. She was large, with thin straw-coloured hair which Nat always wanted to style for her. Her eyes bulged slightly, but they were kind – blue and kind.

The two women hugged on the doorstep. When Nat didn't let go, Tina said: 'Woah, Nat, feels like you needed that. Let's go in and shut the door, you're letting all the cold in.'

When they pulled apart, Nat felt ashamed of the tears running down her cheeks. She pulled her hanky from the sleeve of her cardy and wiped them away.

'What's wrong, love?' said Tina, shutting the door behind her.

Nat shook her head.

'Come on, come and sit down. I'll make you a cup of tea. I bought some mince pies. It's nearly Christmas.'

couldn't quite believe he was there. 'Come in, you look frozen through.'

He glanced left and right, down the miserable, grizzled street. A double-decker bus, a green and beige No.35, rumbled past, its great tyres spreading brown slush. For a moment, an armoured vehicle with wheels at the front and tracks at the back was in his mind's eye, then gone. He opened the gate and hurried up the path.

Lily stood aside as she ushered him into the warmth of her home.

'What were you doing out there? Look at the state of you, you're soaked through!'

She was a slender Scottish woman with a pale complexion and long black hair cut straight across the fringe. She was pretty. Ray certainly knew how to choose them.

'Ray – Theo's here,' she shouted back down the hall.

Theo's friend appeared in the doorway of the front room. 'You look like you've been in the bath, mate!' he said. 'What you up to?'

'Just a bit of shopping,' said Theo, rustling the bag. 'Christmas decorations.'

'Didn't bring a brolly?'

Theo smirked. 'No.'

'Go in and sit down with him, I'll bring you some tea,' said Lily. She noticed the cuts on Theo's head and mouth. 'You took a bashing in that scrap last night, too, didn't you, love?' she said, raising her fingers to his forehead but not quite touching the wound. 'I don't know, you boys…'

Theo nodded. Best not to go into the details about the car accident as well, he thought. The figure in the road, it was him, surely, in the uniform…

'That's a nasty one,' she said, continuing to look at the cut on his forehead. 'Bloody troublemakers. You'd think it was 1946, not '76, wouldn't you? Some people just won't let it lie.'

'It's nothing,' said Theo.

'I'll get you a towel, you can dry your hair.'

He followed Ray into the front room.

'You're drenched to the bone, mate,' said the swarthy man. 'Sit down.'

Theo sat in one of the patterned armchairs, beside a corner lamp with a tasselled shade. He set the bag down beside him, noticing a frizzy length of string on the floor. Wondered if their ginger tom, Bertie, might be under the chair.

'So, to what do we owe the pleasure, my friend?' said Ray, sitting in the chair opposite him. They didn't have a sofa, just four armchairs and a padded stool by a walnut coffee table. There was no TV either, but they did have a wooden-panelled Bang and Olufsen hi-fi in the alcove near the window. All Ray's records and cassettes were neatly shelved below it, the Frankie Valli, Glen Campbell, Major Harris, all the American country and R'n'B as well as a few Brits too, the Kinks and of course the Beatles.

A Nazi ghost brought me here. What could he say?

'Just thought I'd pop by, check how you were faring. After last night.'

Ray lifted his right hand, showed him the split skin on two of his knuckles. 'Stings like hell this morning,' he said. 'Lily insisted on an iodine soak.'

Theo winced in sympathy. 'Nat gave me the same when I got home.'

'Don't remember you getting that cut on the head,' said Ray.

Theo reached up instinctively, felt the scab of it. He was about to say something when Lily came in and handed him a towel.

'There you go. Dry yourself up. I'll bring you a cuppa.'

'Thanks.'

He rubbed the thin towel vigorously over his scalp, avoiding the cut and the bruises around it.

'Now you look like Gil Scott-Heron, in the old days,' Ray joked. Theo pushed his hair down. 'That's better…'

Theo pulled his tobacco out of his pocket and prised the tin open with his thumb.

'So why are you really here?' said Ray.

Nat

'I keep seeing… things.'

The table was only small and Tina, leaning forward on her elbows with a steaming mug of tea in her hands, was almost on top of her.

The woman raised her eyebrows. 'What do you mean?'

Nat looked up at her, then back at her hands. 'Like… maybe… ghosts?'

A pause. 'Tell me about it.'

Staring down, Nat said: 'There's this man. He keeps appearing to me…'

'What kind of man?'

'He's a soldier.'

'When do you see him?'

'He… he was here the night before last. Standing staring at me. Right there, by my shoulder,' she gestured. 'When I got up in the night to go to the loo.'

'Oh Nat, how frightening. Did he do anything?'

'No, he just stared at me. But it was horrible. He had some blood… spots of blood on his face. It was horrible!'

'What kind of soldier was he? Like a Roman soldier or something? Or from the war, a Tommy?'

'Yes, he was modern. World War Two. But not a Tommy. I'm sure he's German.'

'A German? Blimey, Nat…'

'I've seen him before, too. He's been… visiting me… for a while.'

'Since when?'

'Years.'

'How many?'

'Eighteen. Since…'

'Since what, Nat?'

'Since Daisy.'

'Shit.'

Nat looked pleadingly into her friend's blue eyes. 'I know.'

'Does Theo see him too?'

'I think so, but not as clearly – or as much – as me. He had a crash last night, coming home on the downs. Said someone was there, in the road. A figure… Oh Tina, I'm really scared. Really, really bloody scared!'

Tina reached forward and gripped her arm. 'I'm helping you, my love,' she said. 'You know I am.'

'Thank you.'

There was a moment's silence. Thoughts battled in Nat's mind. Should she say something else? Tina wasn't one of her oldest friends, she'd only met her a few years back when they were working in Simpson's, the Chemist, but she was the one she felt closest too. Ever since the death of Miriam Bonniface from that terrible skin cancer five years ago.

'Is there something else?' As usual, Tina seemed to read her mind.

'Before you came, there was… someone else… here.'

'Just now?'

'Yes. A woman. A young woman. She… oh!' The force with which she broke surprised her. Nat sobbed and wailed, disappeared into a place of white noise, a place of horrific pain, next time she became aware she was doubled up on her knees and Tina was squeezing her side, rubbing her back, speaking into her neck.

'Nat, darling, it's alright, what is it, Nat, what happened, love, you'll be alright, I'm here…'

Abruptly she sat up, grabbing Tina's hand, feeling the rings, rubbing her fingers.

'I'm OK,' she said. 'I'm alright.'

Tina pulled her chair around so she could sit and hold her hand.

'She…' said Nat. 'She…' She took a deep breath and looked into Tina's face.

'She called me…'

'What did she call you, my love? What did the woman say?'

'She called me Mum.'

Theo

'Just one more shift and then it's Christmas, mate!'

Standing framed with his wife in the door, Ray waved to Theo as he opened the gate and stepped out on to the street.

'Yeah, see you later,' said Theo with a nod, waving back.

The sleet had stopped as he headed back towards the car. The sky was gloomy, heavy and dark. He checked his watch, it was nearly two o'clock. Nat would be worrying like mad, he'd been gone for hours.

As he came back towards Terminus Road he started to worry about Stanley's, whether one of the shop assistants might be coming out, or perhaps that store detective again. He still had the bag with the stolen lights and baubles. He felt even more desolate about having done it now. What a stupid git he could be, sometimes.

He thought back to the appearance of… him. Outside Stanley's. What was that nasty piece of human excrement doing back? Theo wasn't scared. Or maybe a little, after all, it wasn't every day you saw a ghost. But why, after all these years, was the idiot *Obersoldat* here? Was this who Nat had seen? And maybe, the figure in the woods, and the next night, on the road. He couldn't be sure.

And… why did he lead him to Ray's house?

Theo thought back to the chat in Ray's living room, Lily coming in with the tea. He'd considered, really been on the verge of, telling Ray how come he'd appeared, soaked through, outside his house. But then bottled it. How could you talk to a grown man and woman about a thing like that? I came round because a ghost brought me… They'd think he'd gone round the bend. Impulsively, he'd invited them over to dinner that night, for a Chinese. The distraction had worked, changing the subject.

He thought of the flashback, the sense he'd had of being back there in Caen, that horrific incident in the storage room with the machine gunner. Perhaps he *was* going round the bend?

His head ached. Was that just the cold, the hangover? He hoped it wasn't one of his migraines coming on…

He had to get home, needed to see his wife.

Needed the reassurance of Nat.

Nat

'He should be back by now. Theo – where is he?'

Nat looked at the clock on the mantelpiece.

'It takes time, something like that,' said Tina. 'Getting a car out of a ditch with a tractor.'

'Not this much time,' said Nat.

'Perhaps they had to tow him to get it fixed in town?'

Nat shrugged. Her gaze drifted back to Amber, who stared indifferently at the bay windows. Why did she get to have her own chair?

How horrible! Why did she keep having these rotten thoughts about Amber?

'I'll stay with you 'til he gets back.'

'But you can't. Your ticket…'

'I'm sure they'll change it for me.'

'They won't, you know they won't…'

'Leave that to me.'

Nat knew British Rail wouldn't change a ticket, not at this late stage. The trains up to London were always fully booked at this time of year. 'I can't let you miss it. Please…'

'What are you going to do, Nat? About these strange… visions? The ghosts?'

'I'll talk to Theo. Talk to him about them.'

'That's best,' said Tina. 'He'll help you.'

Nat was quiet.

'Is there something you're not telling me?'

The phone rang. Nat stood up, hurried into the hall and picked it up.

'Hello, love, it's me.'

'Theo! Did you get the car out?'

'Yes,' he said. 'I went into town after.'

'So it's running fine, that's a relief.'

'Yes. There's a couple of things need fixing, but I reckon they can wait for the new year. Next paycheck. I'm on my way home now.'

'Good.'

'I popped in to see Ray and Lily. Asked them over for a meal later. Thought we could get a Chinese.'

'Oh.'

'Take our minds off… things.'

'But we haven't got the money for a Chinese…'

'He's insisted on splitting it. You know Ray.'

She was quiet. She did know Ray.

Theo

He was driving home under a pale grey sky, hoping there wouldn't be more snow.

The Beetle was struggling on the hills. There was something wrong with the engine, he knew it. He would have to take her in to Jack's for a check. In the new year. Next wages. As long as she made it into work tomorrow. But snow wouldn't help, wouldn't help at all…

Why was it snowing? Everyone always talked about white Christmases but they hardly ever happened. Once or twice in the sixties, then in '70, but very few otherwise. Was it going to be snow for Christmas this year? It was only two days away. It always sounded like a nice idea, Bing singing his heart out about it in the film, but the reality of snow up here on the downs was shovelling ice off the drive in the freezing cold and astronomical heating bills. And even with the central heating on full there were bits of the house that never properly warmed up.

Still, he would make sure he and Nat had a nice day of it. He'd got them a tree and some decorations – even if dishonestly – and he'd bought her a couple of presents. A silver necklace with amber studs from H. Samuel and the latest Sidney Sheldon. And he'd got them a bottle of Blue Nun for Christmas day and they still had a little whiskey left for appetisers. Bring home a cut of ham and turkey tomorrow evening and Bob was well and truly your uncle…

He slowed down as he headed into a small curving valley. Two sheep had got out through a broken fence and one was half on the road as it tugged away at the grass verge. Theo checked in his rear-view mirror to make sure no one was behind him and slammed on the brakes when he saw a man and a woman sitting in the backseat of the car, both staring at the reflection of his eyes.

Nat

Waiting.

Waiting again.

Tina had had to go, otherwise she wouldn't have had time to get her train up to London, where she was staying with her daughter and son-in-law for Christmas. Nat had told her she would be alright, insisted on it, Theo would be back soon. But as soon as she'd gone, promising to call as she left, Nat had felt the panic, gone to the kitchen, shut herself in again…

Why was she always waiting alone? It's the woman's role in life, her mother had once told her. To wait. In both meanings of the word. For, and on, her man.

But Theo wasn't like that. He did things round the house when he wasn't at work. Washing up, the laundry even. And the dusting, he did that every Sunday. He liked to keep busy, liked things tidy. He didn't cook but what man did? Trixie Parker's husband, Harold, but that was because they ran a restaurant on the seafront and he loved it. He'd lived in Italy for a while, where there were lots of male chefs, she'd heard. Part of the Mediterranean tradition.

Her daughter had visited her. As a grown woman.

Oh my good God.

She felt her breath lock in her chest. Panic. What had happened?

She couldn't breathe. She literally couldn't breathe. She jumped up and ran the tap, filled a glass and drank, gulped it down.

Her daughter! An adult!

She died when she wasn't even one year old.

Oh my God.

How could she stand this? How could she stand it?

She thought about the woman's face, so bright and beautiful, the red lips, pure white skin, a little rouge on the cheeks. And her eyes, clear and green. She was Daisy, but...

How could she be?

How could she be her daughter? Oh, she wished Tina was still with her. Her mind was growing full of doubt again. Mushrooming with doubts, not with little white button mushrooms but with those foul ones, grey, veined, chunky, yellowing in places, feeding off black, dead wood... Oh Lord!

With Tina there, reality, this real world with its steady, predictable things, the mugs, coffee jar, draining board, had all returned, but now they were being taken over again, something inside was pushing itself out, she felt it, like a physical lump inside, a pressure, a pressure of chaos, madness, a demon, like a demon…

A demon of grief.

Madness and grief and…

Guilt.

A demon of guilt.

She was holding her in her arms. Her baby. Her beautiful baby daughter.

Daisy.

They were in the garden of Black Beacon, the second year in their own home, out on the lawn by one of the deck chairs, and it was summer. High summer. High summer on the downs. What a paradise! Heat over all the land, gulls sweeping the sky. The roses that Nat grew and tended carefully were in bloom, their citrus scent wafting through the warm air.

Sublime.

She looked at her baby's face, her closed eyes, the lids buttery and thin, the delicate scooped lashes, gingery, or like the colour of wine. The pink button nose. A whorl of reddish hair on the crown. She wanted to kiss her head but you don't wake a baby in a light sleep. Not if you wanted to preserve the magic, the quiet, the moment.

The moment with her dazzling baby daughter. The girl they thought they'd never have. Not after St. Vith.

But then…

How could she cope with this? Who was that woman at the door? Did children grow in the afterlife? Did they become their adult soul?

Because that was who had visited her today.

The grown soul of her darling baby daughter.

Oh good Lord, sweet Jesus, good God… why had she been given this gift?

This gift before Christmas. She who didn't deserve it.

Oh my Lord Jesus…

The Boy

Theo

This time he wasn't drunk and he didn't crash the car.

Just slammed the brakes and stopped it right there, in the middle of the country road.

Then turned and looked around at them.

Dieter in his Obersoldat uniform, the neat grey tunic with the *V* insignia on the sleeve, the peak cap, with blood spattered on his face, perhaps *Theo's blood*, and those dreadful wounds on his stomach and legs.

And sitting beside him, the woman – Sophie Fischer, whose name he remembered so well, even after all these years – with her white skin and red lips.

*

And then, blinking, blinking, he was back there, back in Köln again.

Early December, 1944. Evening – no, later, night.

Snow on the ground. Bitter cold. Unbearable. Smoking and shivering as he shuffled back in the freezing air, back to the large townhouse where he was barracked. Just seventeen years old.

But somehow, despite everything, the atrocities across Europe, the world, that year – somehow a frosty beauty in the moonlight, illuminating that snowy alley. It took his breath away, the contrast of it, the one emphasizing the other: unbearable beauty on top of unbearable tragedy. It cut his heart.

He was a little drunk, a few too many schnapps in the café, no orders to be ready for battle for a few days, he and his colleagues from the Fifteenth had been drinking with some guys from Sixth Panzer, tank men, and they'd been laughing and exchanging stories from back home… But now he was alone, heading back to yet another makeshift bed for the night. He was feeling sorrowful, thinking about his mother in Kaiserslautern, how worried she must be now that the news of Berne being captured had reached her. Her two older sons both now Prisoners of War – although at least they weren't dead. If only his father were still alive, Theo knew how much she relied on him, passive and impenetrable as he was, with his pipe and paper, the Napoleonic lead soldiers he painted obsessively in his study in his spare time. But even though he was remote, he was a good man, kind, who wouldn't shirk from doing the right thing…

Theo felt a tear pricking his eye as he imagined her alone, stoking the fire with the blackened poker, the one with the brass bear's head, fretting about the war, about her sons. And him, the only one still fighting, who she would only hear from once every two or three months, when he screwed up the resolve to write a letter back to her.

His melancholic mood was shattered by a noise up ahead. Was it a child? A small group appeared from the gloom, two men and a boy. The boy was talking rapidly, his voice rising, piercing the stillness of the alley. He realised he'd been wrong, the person who replied was a woman, her voice, low, reassuring. As the group came closer, Theo saw it was a man on the right, a soldier, and a woman on the left, with the child in between them. The boy kept asking questions, the woman replying evenly, with an occasional teasing lilt to her voice. The man, he realised, was a Wehrmacht soldier, in a peak cap and greatcoat. The woman wore a long winter coat and a small black hat. The breath of all three steamed around them.

'…the doctor?' the boy was saying, in his high, piping voice. Theo guessed he was perhaps nine or ten. He was wearing a blue cap and a grey woollen overcoat.

'That's right,' said the woman. 'Vati will be fine, the doctor is just around…'

'Well, look who it isn't…'

Theo had been watching the boy's face, the pale sheen of his cheeks in the moonlight, the mole on his cheek, thinking how similar it was to his brother Jürgen's, when the man spoke.

'Theo Webber!'

He looked up at the soldier.

'Dieter!' he said. With his attention on the striking woman and the boy, Theo hadn't recognised the Obersoldat who he and his mates tended to steer clear of. Too arrogant, too much of a propaganda puppet. Overbearing and unpleasant with it.

Now, Theo looked properly at the two adults and the child.

Dieter smiled. 'We found Tomas here wandering aimlessly on the Rathaus Platz,' he said. 'His father is sick at home and he was trying to find a doctor.'

'So that's where we're taking him,' said the woman.

'I recognise you,' said Theo. 'Aren't you Sophie Fischer?'

The woman smiled. Her lips were beautiful but her teeth were a little crooked. 'I am,' she said. 'Have we met?'

You grew up fast in the war. Before his conscription in January, he had been working for one of the *HJ*, the Hitler Youth, magazines as a sub-editor. He had an appetite for journalism, for telling a story, for revealing, or at least interpreting, truth. And he liked entertaining different perspectives, something which didn't always endear him to his elders and betters. Much of the HJ activity was anathema to him, he wasn't into the forest hikes, boorish songs and outdoor pursuits – although he was an enthusiastic footballer and enjoyed the matches between area groups – but he found his niche in the magazine.

The articles he wrote, juvenile and shameful to him now, explored ideas about the *Herrenrasse*, the Nazi concept of the Master Race, with its semi-mythical origins in Atlantis. His style was to highlight inconsistencies, gaps and occasional absurdities – but always within an overall context of reinforcement. His editor occasionally rejected his pieces, but more often than not took them, if a little anxiously. But his readers – small in number as they were – liked them, and his feedback was mostly positive. Like him, most people were secretly sceptical of what they were told by the Ministry of Propaganda but, also like him, most wanted to believe. To find a way to believe, at least some of it.

Through his articles, he found a way of speaking to this small and largely silent audience.

Sophie Fischer was one of the famous *proper* journalists he admired. She worked for one of the established nationals, the magazine *Neue Morgendämmerung*. At the start of the war she'd written extensively on the ideas of the Reich, focusing on interviews with popular philosophers and artists such as Rosenberg and Breker. Latterly, with the changes in the war, the switch to defence, she'd become more focused on motivational articles, on how there was still a prospect for the Wehrmacht to achieve ultimate victory. Her photo appeared beside all her articles – he would recognise her anywhere.

'Oh, you've seen my work,' she added quickly, there, now, in that snow-filled midnight alleyway. Leading a young boy to the doctors, with Dieter Anders, no less. 'Yes, that's me,' she added.

The boy appeared confused between them.

Theo gazed at her. 'I...' he was going to say *used to be*, then checked himself. 'I'm a fan,' he said.

'How nice,' she said, with a small smile.

It was obvious she wanted to move on.

'We'll see you soon, Theo,' said Dieter. And then all three were gone, moving on through the thick snow trapped between the narrow walls of the alley.

And now, here they were once again, after all those years, sitting behind him in his Volkswagen Beetle.

And he had just one question for them.

Nat

It was getting dark.

Nat stood up and stared out of the kitchen window above the washing machine, out at the grim, featureless fields surrounding Black Beacon, the fields that smothered the top of a down. A Sussex Down. *Down*. And yes, they bloody well could make you feel down, she thought. Terribly down, especially in this dreary winter light, covered with a muted grey snowfall, empty everywhere, as far as the eye could see. Off to the severe horizon, beyond which lay more bleak downs one way and cliffs the other, the cold white cliffs of the Seven Sisters dropping to the iron-grey sea. So many suicides up there, sometimes as many as one a week. A place barren and desolate enough not to trouble you with distractions when you'd decided you'd had enough of it all, when you wanted to take that one small step to finish it off.

Nat!

What was she thinking? She loved the downs! She forced to mind the weekend visits she and her dad had made on the bus up from town, the walks they'd done in summer, spotting butterflies, the Duke of Burgundy, yellow Brimstone, the adorable Adonis Blue. The place she'd first met her handsome husband with his PoW co-workers, the place they'd strolled with their newborn Daisy clutched tight against Theo's open shirt, twisting her baby fingers in the dark hair of his chest...

She loved the downs!

How could you feel two opposite things about one place? The weather. The weather made all the difference. And a visit by...

Oh good grief, how could her nerves cope with this? She needed him back, where was he, what was he doing, it was nearly four o'clock for goodness' sake...

And she had to tell him. Tell him his daughter was here. The beautiful, pure soul of his grown daughter. In a visitation.

Was she having one of those things, those mental breakdown things? Her heart had been bursting with joy only a few hours earlier and now...

Theo

'What did you do with him?'

It was gloomy in the back of the car, late afternoon now, very little light coming in through the small, rounded back windows. The two glared at him from under their hats.

'The boy? What did you do with that boy?'

And then he was remembering the kid's face, that inquisitive freshness, the openness, the trust…

And a few days later, when the bombs were raining from the skies, nonchalantly obliterating the lives and beauty of Köln, he'd been trotting through the wide Konig-Baudouin Platz, rifle held loose at his side, and he'd seen that notice, no, two notices, on the ornate black street lamps, the notices about a missing child, and he'd thought, no, no one posts anything like that now, not when every child is lost in this war, when every soul is lost…

But then, with a stab in his chest, he'd made the connection with the boy and the journalist and the vaguely ridiculous Obersoldat and thought, no, surely no…

He should have done something about it. He had sworn to do something about it.

But the bombs and then the next day the move out to Sankht Vith and the battle starting and, oh, that old soldier they all loved, his name was Paul but everyone called him Opa, he was older than Theo's father when he died – he'd lost half his face to a bullet in that battle… and then the chaos, the chaos after…

Oh Christ.

'What did you do with him?' he said. Shouted.

He could see a slick, half-smile on the woman's face, her lips red like a knife cut, Dieter regarding him appraisingly, as if Theo's emotion was nothing more than a show laid on for his personal entertainment…

And he thought things then, as the gloom swelled on the downs, sunk slowly round the Volkswagen skewed in the road, Theo thought of his own miraculous daughter, Daisy, her darling fingers with the pale half-moons of nail, how they curled around his brown thumb, the gap in her mouth when her lips opened in a little smile… and he didn't use the word miraculous lightly, of course, she really was astonishing, a wonder, something that should never have happened, *almost* should not have happened, not after the blast outside Sankht Vith, the blast that had…

Aye-aye-aye-aye-aye, why was he thinking all this now?

And then something dropped, he realised why Dieter had led him to his friend's house in Eastbourne, why he and Sophie were here now, how it all fitted together…

'Dieter, you bastard!' He lunged across the seat at the foul spectre in the back of the car who, of course, was not there.

Maybe never was there.

He got trapped, awkwardly, in between the front seats, feeling the pressure on the bruises he'd suffered in the accident last night, wondering what in God's name was happening to him, what was happening…?

Nat

She sighed at the sight of the rounded cream roof of the car in the valley below Black Beacon, semi-concealed by the cut of the road so it looked like… a boil. A bright, yellow boil in the grim, snow-covered landscape. Oh, for goodness' sake, Nat, stop thinking these thoughts!

She wanted to run out and meet him.

But waited. As always.

Nat waited.

*

When he came in, shrouded by a cloak of cold air, she could tell at once he was in a mood. A strange mood. Very strange. It made her anxious. More anxious.

He brushed her off as she tried to grab him, kiss his cheek, wanting to hold him. Needing to hold him, right now.

'What is it?' she said desperately, as he dropped his plastic bag on the floor and swept off his sheepskin jacket and shoved it on the coat stand.

'Nah…' was all he muttered, striding off into the kitchen.

She needed to tell him what had happened, about Daisy, their daughter, how she had come back, the miracle of it…

Instead, she walked slowly into the living room and sat down on the sofa and began to cry.

Outside, she heard him banging, clashing cupboards. The drink cupboard. He was getting himself a drink. She couldn't sit still, she stood up, strode over to Amber and picked her up, put her down again, the doll's head sagged over, Nat moved her upright, she sagged again against the cushion, Nat picked her up and hurled her across the room into the bay area, just missing the Christmas tree.

Theo came in, empty glass in hand.

'What was that?' he said.

'Nothing!'

As soon as he saw her tears he put the glass on the coffee table and took her in his arms.

'What is it?' he said. 'What, Nat?'

She sobbed recklessly against his shirt. The dampness spread quickly.

'What is it?' He looked at the doll, lying face down on the red carpet.

'She came…' Nat whispered.

'What?'

'She came…'

'What did you say?'

'I said she came.'

'Who? Tina?'

'Daisy.'

'What?'

'Daisy came.'

He eased her away, holding her by the arms so he could see her face clearly.

'Daisy who?'

'Daisy – our girl. Your daughter. She came. She was here. In our home…'

Theo

Despite his two recent larcenies, he knew he was a good man, a practical man, a level-headed man – God, he'd lived through the bloody war, hadn't he, on the losing side no less, almost been blown to kingdom come, all without being crushed, defeated – but this... this was doing his head in.

Whatever *this* was.

Them. And what they wanted to do. What they wanted him to know and... what was their motive?

'What do you mean?' he said.

'She came to the door,' said Nat. 'She's grown up. Theo – she's all grown up...'

'Don't say that,' he said.

'She is, Theo, she's a woman now, a beautiful young woman...'

'Don't, Nat.'

'She came in and – and do you know... do you know what she called me?'

'Nat...'

'Mum. She called me Mum. And she talked about you... her dad.'

'Oh God, Nat...'

Despite his worry, his anger, despite everything, he pressed her against his chest and closed his eyes.

The phone rang. It must have broken the devilish spell on her because she pulled away from him and went out to the hall. He heard her talking to someone. Lily? She sounded in control, at least, not... hysterical.

He saw Amber, lying on her front, her hair cast across her turned face. Had Nat thrown her? Was that what the crack was? He went over, turned on the gold lamp, stooped and lifted the doll.

When he smoothed back her hair he saw that there was a crack on her hairline. Not bad, but deep enough to show the peachy edge of the rubber. He pushed it with his thumb. Why did she hurl Amber?

Amber...

He thought about those two in the car. Those... *demons*.

He thought about the things that had come to his mind as they sat there, staring at each other, like a scene out of one of his Tom West paperbacks, the cowboy gunslingers all sizing each other up before the inevitable yank at holsters. Who was going to draw first?

Alongside the boy, the posters, something else had resurfaced, the awful memory of...

The Panzerschreck moment, when his entire life hung in the balance, poised between his forefinger and the metal trigger. The Sherman, white snow showering up around its black tracks. Its slippery, relentless momentum as it ground its way up the road, its flanks strewn with netting, sandbags, a long-handled shovel strapped to the side. And up on top, that American commander with his goggles on his helmet, perched on the edge of the cupola, arm resting casually on the stock of his mounted machine gun.

Fire! *Erschiess ihn!*

Dieter. Shut up, Dieter. *Halt den Mund.*

Shoot, Theo, fire now, it's the right time, fire for God's sake, blow that American fucker to…

Shut the fuck up.

A bird flew up then, black, a crow or raven. Rare to see birds anywhere near the battlefield, that's why he remembered it. Black against the snow. The commander shouting into his radio, pausing amid the growl and rumble of the tracks. His head turning…

Now, Theo, fire, you spineless fool…

Shut up, the tank will pass soon, Dieter, shut up, our best chance is the back, to hit the back…

You bloody idiot, Dieter. You bloody idiot.

He could see the commander's face, pale, verging on white, sickly-looking in the winter chill, turning towards them, lying there, pressed up against that frozen pipe.

The moment of cold certainty when he realised he'd been seen, clocked, the way the tank commander's fluid movement ceased, seemingly countering the whole motion of the tank beneath him, the two staring at each other across the sights of that long metal bazooka...

Like two Wild West gunfighters.

Exactly like them.

And then all back to real-life speed, velocity, the tug of the trigger, the puff of acrid smoke in his face and the frenzied hail of bullets in response, whirring, clunking, and then...

Then.

The explosion.

Flame, whiteness. Whiteness in the white.

Snow on snow.

The white and its hidden roar, the roar that came from within it, like a secret message.

The roar that destroyed Dieter, the futile, evil bastard.

The roar that, in a way, destroyed Theo too. Which is what had come to his mind, sitting there in his stopped Volkswagen, staring at those despicable Nazi spectres, the spectres that stared back at him.

The ghouls who didn't give a damn about that boy, who just wanted Theo to know that...

Staring at the blackness that had filled the bay windows, he heard Nat saying goodbye, goodbye to Tina, and hanging up the phone. He turned and stared at her as she came back into the room. She looked at him, then at the doll he was holding half-heartedly, a querying look on his face.

'Why...?' he said.

She shook her head slowly. When he looked at her face it looked like she had lost the power in all her muscles, there was no lift there at all. He realised how much our daily expressions require effort, the hollowness that descends when we truly relax, give in.

'What time are they here?' she said.

'Ray and Lily?' He looked at his watch, a black-faced Junkers with white strikes that he'd bought one summer at the end of the sixties, the time he'd visited his brothers in Kaiserslautern. 'Uh – not long,' he said. 'They said they'd come early, because of tomorrow's shift. Half-five.'

'It's an early one?'

'Yes.'

'Let's tidy up and get the table laid,' said Nat.

'I wish I hadn't bloody invited them,' said Theo.

'Why did you?'

'I... Let's just get through the evening, get it over with.'

'Let's do that.'

He watched as she turned and walked out and thought he'd never in nearly thirty years felt such distance between them.

The Chinese

Nat

The stupid thing was, all she was trying to do was get the cutlery out from the bloody sideboard drawer.

But her fingers would not obey her brain. One moment working, the next fumbling like they lacked bone and muscle. Like they were made of jelly. Just four forks, four knives and four spoons – how hard could it be? But they were slipping into each other, she had too many spoons, the knives were upside down, then she remembered she needed serving spoons for the trays too, her hands were shaking, she thought she had the right amount of knives but when she put them down there were only three, how could you count something so small wrong? Fleetingly, she remembered handing over the incorrect change in the tearoom, all those years ago in that café with Klaus, Theo, and Miriam. That small tearoom with the purple walls and the dinky green side plates in Terminus Road, *Rita's*, Rita was a character, she recalled, quite rude a lot of the time to her customers but they all seemed to love her in spite of it, and of course she was dead, dead now from those strokes, four strokes, each one almost six months to the day after the other…

Nat banged the fourth knife down sharply on the wooden table beside the place mat with its photograph of glossy violets, denting the varnish.

She sat down, pushed her eyebrows with the palms of her hands.

Why was he in a mood? Why had he invited them? He never thought, that was his trouble. Stupid… *No…*

'Amber!' she said it out loud. Stood up, looked at the tambour clock on the sideboard, saw it was nearly twenty-five past the hour, hurried back into the living room leaving the table only half laid.

Amber was back on her chair. The dent on her forehead showed, the rough pink crack in the rubber.

Nat hurried over to the doll, picked her up and pushed her fingers along the line, hoping she could ease out the dent in the rubber.

She couldn't. Trying to pull up one edge, to get her finger under it so she could prise it out, she jammed it in further.

There was a tap on the door, their feeble brass knocker.

'Shit!'

She looked around wildly. Knelt down on the red carpet and threw the doll under the sofa.

Stood up, brushed her skirt down, and headed out into the hall.

'They're here, Theo,' she shouted up the stairs, thinking he must have gone to change his shirt. She opened the door.

'Nat, love!'

It was Lily came in first, the sweet meaty smell of the Chinese wafting in with her from the bag she was holding. Lily reached out one arm, managed to encircle Nat's neck and kiss her cheek.

Then moved aside and there he was, coming up fast behind his wife.

Ray Teal.

With his Italian complexion, his dark wavy hair and rich brown eyes, shining at her.

'How are you, Nat?' he asked and she felt a moment of blind panic, as if her knees would buckle.

'Oh…' was all she managed to say as he moved to kiss her on the lips. She turned her head a little so he kissed her cheek instead. Ray smiled and moved past her into the hall, with his wife.

'Theo's getting changed,' she said, although she didn't know if it was true. 'Come in the…'

She was thinking, the dining room, get them in there straight away, then she wouldn't have to… but they had already gone straight into the living room, as usual, Ray carrying his bottle of Blue Nun and Lily passing back the bag with the Chinese and telling her to pop it in the oven to keep it warm, which was just as normal, so they could all have an aperitif to start with, a glass of wine, just as normal.

Just as normal.

Except nothing now, nothing at all, was normal.

She could feel it in her bones.

Feel them cracking.

*

She hurried the foil trays into the oven, then collected some wine glasses and a corkscrew from the sideboard in the dining room.

On her way back into the living room she shouted again to Theo. Thinking again, what kind of mood was he in, why had he been so off with her…?

Lily was sitting on the sofa and Ray was standing by the tree in the bay when she came back in.

'Need a few lights for this,' he said. 'Fairy lights…'

'Let me help you with those,' said Lily, taking two glasses by their squat stems and setting them down on the coffee table.

Nat threw a glance at the empty armchair as Ray bent down and picked up the Blue Nun. He held out his hand to her and she looked at him uncomprehendingly.

'Wine's not going to open itself,' he said, grinning.

'Oh, yes,' she said and handed the corkscrew to him.

He looked at the chair.

'Amber move on at last?' he said, brushing his mouth with the cuff of his sleeve.

She kept quiet. Didn't know what to say.

Lily gave her a look of concern. 'Sit down, Nat, you look rushed off your feet,' she said in her gentle Scots accent, patting the sofa beside her.

She sat down for something to do. Ray continued to look at the armchair. She felt her cheeks burn.

'It's bloody freezing out,' said Lily. 'Car was slipping all over the place on the way up. You want to make sure you don't get snowed in up here. Still, at least we might get a white Christmas!' She gave a little pretend shiver of her shoulders, then looked at her husband and said: 'Hurry up, Ray, we need a drink to warm the cockles!'

He turned, coming back from his thoughts. With a smile, he dug the corkscrew into the cork, began to twist.

Theo appeared at the door in a clean white shirt, the folds at the top of his sleeves visible where he wore elasticated bands to shorten them. He'd never fitted a normal shirt. Nat used to ask him to *hold her in his little arms*, an affectionate tease.

Now he smelt sharp and handsome, a splash of the Old Spice making the difference.

'Just in time,' he said, reaching for a glass as Ray poured it.

'Nice tree, mate,' said Ray.

'Haven't had time to put on those decorations I got earlier,' said Theo, glancing at Nat.

With his wine, Theo glanced around for somewhere to sit. Ray was near Lily, likely to sit between her and Nat any moment on the sofa. He noticed the empty armchair.

'Oh – her ladyship has left the room,' he said.

Nat felt a flicker of horror. He'd never referred to Amber like that before, what a strange turn of phrase. What had got into him?

'I'll have her seat, then,' he concluded, and sat down heavily in the chair. There was an unhealthy cracking sound underneath. 'Whoops,' he said. 'She must have been heavier than she looked.'

Ray and Lily laughed.

'That sounded a bit serious,' said Lily. 'You might want to get up and check it?'

Theo looked over each side of the chair. 'Seems to be holding,' he said.

'Probably one of the springs,' said Ray.

Nat took a long slug of wine. 'How is the car, love?' she said.

Theo looked at her.

'Something wrong with the Volkswagen?' said Ray.

'No, nothing much,' said Theo. 'Had a little encounter with a ditch on the way home last night.'

'You didn't tell us,' said Lily.

Theo shrugged. 'Just one of those things,' he said, directing his gaze at Nat, looking at her a little too long. She frowned.

'What time shall we eat?' she said, a complete non-question as it was always after the drink.

'Yes, I'm starving,' said Lily. 'I'm ready as soon as we've had this one.'

Nat could feel the Scots woman was picking up on something in her mood. She was sympathetic like that. Or was it empathetic? Whatever it was, she was trying to help her out.

'Shall I go and get it on the table now?' Nat said.

'Yes, why don't you do that?' said Theo.

She stood up, holding her glass.

'I'll come with you,' said Lily, with half a smile.

Theo

He was rubbing his thumb against his forefinger for a while before he realised he could have a fag.

Ray was chatting on about Brian Hart, one of the night shift managers whose parents had both been diagnosed with cancer on the run up to Christmas, how it was going to be a grim time for the whole family, and whilst Theo liked Brian, a quiet, sensible bloke from the Wirral, he couldn't help glancing up at Ray and thinking about the ghosts in the back of his car, because that's why they were there, weren't they, after all, he couldn't deny it now, they wanted him to think these thoughts, these awful thoughts…

He popped open his battered tin of Old Holborn and fiddled a Rizla out of its green card pack.

'…and it's not like Sheila hasn't got her own problems with her health, and with their little Teddy…'

'Hm.'

'You alright, mate?'

Theo looked up. Ray was watching him carefully, with care. Those steady brown eyes, with the thick black lashes. A bit like Elvis. He was a good-looking chap, Theo supposed. But now, a little… smug. Theo saw it.

'The fight shake you up a bit?'

Theo nodded slightly.

'Or is it the other thing you mentioned? Nat…?'

Theo grimaced, rolling his fag. He was feeling something hot in the front of his head, an emotion that sucked up his powers of speech. He was a quiet man, at the best of times.

'Want to talk about it, mate? Man to man. They'll be in the kitchen for a minute or two yet…'

Theo stood up, tapping the pocket of his grey trousers. 'Must have left my matches in the car,' he said and walked out.

The wind was howling when he stepped outside in his shirt. He hurried over to the car, clutching his sides, it was so bitter. He opened the car door – he never locked it out here, there was no point – and saw his matches on the passenger seat.

He picked them up with a glance at the back seats, empty now, but he saw them – saw *them*, in his mind's eye.

'You bastards,' he said and stood upright, slamming the door.

He stopped, looking up at the night sky.

It might be nearing a gale up here on the downs, but there was no denying, it was an astonishing place. The moon was obscured by a dusty cloud, but overhead the stars were white and sharp, fighting for their places amid the near-black dome of the sky. All around were broad, crystalline hills, stretching out into the darkness, pocked with grey patches of scrub and trees. It was icy, he was going numb with it, but nonetheless he thought suddenly about the three wise men, navigating by the stars nearly two millennia ago, in a hot country far away from here. It was nearing holy night and he was full of power.

But not good power, a frustration, anger, welling up inside. He hurried back into the house.

*

They were already in the dining room when he shut the front door against the wind. For a moment he stood against the radiator, trying to warm up. It was awe-inspiring outside, but the gale had blown every ounce of his bodily warmth away across the downs.

He could hear them laughing, Lily, Ray, then Nat. He went upstairs quickly, found himself his warm brown jumper and tugged it on. Then came back down and into the dining room, lit brightly by the ceiling lamp with its spun glass shade like a tipped-up urn.

The sweet and sour smelled good. He forgot about the fag, sat down opposite Nat and began to tuck in.

'...two point three billion pounds,' said Ray emphatically. 'Two. Point. Three. *Billion* pounds.'

'They're going to have to cut services to pay it back,' said Lily. 'All those nurses and doctors…'

'No, he's ruled out the NHS,' said Ray. 'But I never thought we'd see the day when we went to the IMF with our begging bowl. Jesus wept.'

'Didn't have any choice,' said Theo.

'There's always a choice,' said Ray.

'I don't understand it,' said Nat. 'We were doing so well a few years ago, where's all the money gone?'

'Who's a silly billy, then?' said Ray, shrugging his shoulders and doing a passable imitation of the Chancellor, Denis Healey. 'Sooner we get that bunch out…'

'Bad decisions,' said Lily, popping a lump of batter glistening with orange sauce into her mouth.

They all laughed at the obviousness of that.

'Still, we're going to have a good Christmas,' said Ray.

'We've all earned it, that's for sure,' said Lily.

Theo was going to say something but kept shtum. He heaped a spoonful of egg fried rice on to his plate.

'You two doing anything special?' asked Lily.

Theo and Nat looked at each other.

'Just the two of us in Black Beacon,' said Theo.

'We're going over to Mike and his girlfriend,' said Lily.

'How's that going?' said Nat.

'Very well,' said Lily, grinning. 'Two years next February.'

'Hearing wedding bells soon,' said Ray.

'Imagine you a grandad!' said Lily.

Theo snorted. Everyone looked at him.

Ray raised an eyebrow. 'Are you alright, mate?' he said. 'You looked a bit out of sorts when you came round earlier…'

'Ach, I dunno,' said Theo, glancing off at the window. The curtains weren't pulled and Nat had used a stencil to snow spray *Merry Christmases* and angels all over it. He looked back.

'What happened to Amber?' he said, staring at Nat.

'Amber? What…?' she said. Something fell from underneath her stomach, something that held up her world. She clenched her muscles, fearing it might mean a loss of control, something horribly embarrassing.

'What do you mean, love?' she said, grimacing.

Lily looked at her with concern. Ray was watching Theo, but he looked anxious too.

'Come on,' said Theo, 'she sits on that chair for eighteen years and today you take her off and chuck her across the room. Where is she? Or, should I say, it?'

'Theo… you're frightening me,' Nat whispered.

'She's only a doll, mate,' said Ray. His voice was dry, quieter than usual, as if his throat was parched. 'Have a drink, relax.'

Lily was looking at him but his eyes remained fixed on Theo.

'Yes, she was a very nice thought of yours,' said Theo, tight lipped.

Ray went quiet.

'I was just holding her,' said Nat. 'I dropped her and now she's got a small fracture. So I put her away. That's all, love.' She looked at Theo imploringly.

'Ray — what is it?' said Lily, touching her husband's arm.

He looked at her and shrugged but Theo noticed how his face was oddly puffy, his eyes wide and cheeks sagging all of a sudden. Out of sorts himself now, wasn't he?

There was a clunk and everyone looked round to see Nat had knocked her glass over. Trails of wine were spreading quickly over the white tablecloth and around the foil trays of food.

There was fluster, and a rush to clear it all up.

Nat

'Are you sure you're alright, Nat?'

She nodded and Lily gave her a hug.

'Call me tomorrow,' Lily said into her ear. Then turned and followed her husband out into the blustery night.

Nat shut the door.

She turned and faced the empty hall. Theo had gone back into the living room. Her arms hung down by her sides.

She was not alright.

Images flickered at the edge of her vision, the soldier in the mirror, leering over her shoulder, his face spattered with blood, the broken doll, the smiling woman with the beautiful lips and uneven teeth, her *daughter*…

And now this. The past rearing its damning, ugly – so ugly – head.

How could she be alright? How could she?

She should go in there and talk to him, her husband, the man she had spent the last twenty-seven years of her life with, the man she loved like a part of her body, a part of her soul…

She turned and clutched the banister, stiltedly began to climb the stairs.

'Going to bed already?'

She froze. No *love*, no *duck*. *Going to bed, duck?* Slowly, she turned her head to see him standing there, in the doorway of the living room. Dishevelled. Glass in hand.

'Yes. I'm tired.'

'It's been a long day.'

'It's been a long day,' she repeated.

They stared at each other across the hall. She felt her stomach churn. She wasn't used to hostility. Not from him.

'Why don't you come up too, dear?' she said.

'I'm going to have another one of these,' he said, looking down at his glass. 'Why don't you join me?'

She shook her head.

He said something quietly. All she caught was the word *missing*.

'What, love?' she said.

'Nothing.' He paused. Then looked up at her and she gripped the banister harder as she saw the animosity in his eyes. 'I know,' he said.

She shook her head quickly again, like trying to get a fly away from her face. 'What?' she whispered.

'It's all… aye, aye… it's all falling into place…'

'What?' she said again, the desperation like galloping horses in her head. Thunder and tumult.

'The doll, why he bought…'

She watched him, immobile, unable to do anything else.

'He took me to his house…'

'Theo, you've had a lot to…'

'Shut up!'

She gasped and her whole frame shuddered as he strode across the hall to stand at the bottom of the steps, just beneath her. He rubbed his left ear vigorously with the palm of his hand, something she knew he did when he was drunk and his tinnitus was back.

'Tell me it's not true,' he said and she saw the anguish in his eyes and wanted to vanish, be gone, never have to deal with this. Never have to say anything, to erase it all, erase the past.

'What's not true?' she said, knowing at once it was the weakest, most spineless thing she could say and hating herself for it. She couldn't even rise to the occasion.

'That Ray… Ray was the father of…'

Our child, she knew he was about to say *our child*.

'Her!' he finished, and the cold severance of the word shattered her, she felt her knees buckling and she sat quickly on the step, it was all she could do not to collapse forward into him.

Normally he would have helped her in such a state, but he simply said:

'Did you sleep with Ray Teal? Yes or no?'

She couldn't look at him, couldn't look up at his face just above her now. But she felt it there, blazing, like a dark sun. She shrivelled.

'Oh, it all makes sense now,' he said. 'Why couldn't I see it? What an idiot, what a fucking idiot I am…'

'No,' she said. 'Theo…'

'You…' She held her breath, knowing she wouldn't cope if he used certain words against her. Not now. Not ever. '*Schlampe*…'

He turned and disappeared into the living room.

*

Later, when he finally came in and switched on the bedroom light she was still wide awake, listening to the gale outside.

But she pretended to be asleep, lying on her side, facing away from him. She could hear him banging around, taking off his clothes, breathing heavily through his nose. He smoked a lot more when he was drunk, which brought the catarrh up on his chest. She could hear it catching there, setting up blockages in his lungs, making his breath whistle. The smell of alcohol combined with burnt, stale tobacco seeped across the bedcover.

There was a clumping sound and she heard him mutter: 'Aye, aye, aye, aye…'

Eventually he fell into bed, bouncing her on the springs. He coughed loudly, painfully. Her heart was beating so fast she worried he would hear it. With her back to him, she felt oddly vulnerable, exposed. What if…? No, not her Theo.

He quickly settled down.

When she heard his breathing start to even and deepen, a short while later, she climbed out of bed carefully and turned off the main light. Then, realising she needed the loo, she felt a moment of tortured panic.

Did she dare go to the bathroom? What if the soldier was there again? There was only so much she could take, so much she could handle…

She wished she had a pot in the bedroom, like when she was a little girl. She remembered how her mother had made her empty it every morning, even though she hated the smell, the very idea of it. Remembered the one time she tripped and spilt the whole thing on the landing. How her father, good, gentle man that he usually was, had beaten her in a flash of rage. The corridor had smelt for days after, despite her mother scouring it with bleach and water. Perhaps that had been the start of Nat's lifelong obsession with germs? Theo teased her for the way she was always scouring the kitchen with Vim, making sure the surfaces were spotless. Did it all go back to that one episode of shame?

She was distracting herself with memories. Again.

She lifted her long pink robe from the back of the door and wrapped it around herself. She glanced back at Theo, her husband, the man sleeping in the bed. She felt giddy, wondering if she might be physically sick. Then, tentatively, she made her way down the landing to the bathroom.

The tiled floor was freezing, she'd forgotten to put on her slippers. She pulled the light cord, glanced at the cabinet mirror instinctively, then looked sharply down at the black seat of the toilet. Quickly sat and did her business, shutting her eyes and humming the Wizzard song, the one about wishing it was Christmas every day, making sure she wouldn't hear anything else.

Still she heard the wind outside, rushing past Black Beacon. It was so windy and reckless up here on the Downs. Reckless?

Christmas every day. How strange that would be. How very, very strange…

She kept her head down as she washed her hands under the cold water tap with the yellowed bar of Camay, determined not to look up in the mirror. Determined not to feel anything, sense any presence in the tiny room besides her own…

Something, a skipped heartbeat, made her glance up at the mirror.

Nothing.

Or rather, no one. There was no one there.

She twisted the towel around her hands and hurried back to the bedroom.

Theo was snoring now, the full drone, and he had sprawled across her side of the bed. She squeezed herself in under the blankets, on her side, so as to take up as little room as possible. She knew that even if she bashed into him he wouldn't wake, not after such a long day, not with so much wine inside him.

Not now everything was changed.

But still, she didn't want to risk it.

Maybe there would be a way through all this tomorrow.

Maybe.

She shut her eyes to the brightness of a thousand anxious thoughts. Sleep would be a long time coming, if ever, on this night before Christmas Eve.

The Walk in the Snow

Theo

He was out in the dark next morning, doing his best to ignore his crashing hangover and get to work.

That was two heavy nights on the drink, plus a fight, a car crash, the incomprehensible reappearance of Dieter Anders and Sophie Fischer – and then, last night, the reckoning up.

After all these years.

He just had to get through the day. At least the pain of the hangover was keeping the other, deeper pain away. The pain of knowing.

Knowing his life was a delusion.

There was wet, sleety snow falling at 5.30am as he approached the Beetle with hunched shoulders. He ducked into the car and brushed the sleet off his coat, pulled out the choke. Puffed on the rollup in the corner of his mouth to try and give him some focus, some mental clarity. Because everything was muffled, everything was aching.

The car groaned hard, in fits and bursts, as he turned the key. She didn't want to start. Who could blame her?

He stopped, inhaled on the rollie again, then filled the cabin with smoke. His stomach was sore, acidy, he should have shoved a slice of bread and butter down to soak up the booze that was no doubt still stewing in his gut.

He tried the ignition again. More struggling mechanics.

'Come on…' he said, leaning forward on the wheel, any movement better than sitting still in this freeze. With such desolate thoughts.

He left her for the best part of a minute after that, so she wouldn't flood. Stared out of the windscreen as weak, white blotches swung from the dark and struck it. So dark here. So dark…

God, his head.

God, his wife. His *life*.

Third time, she started and he couldn't help but grin and pat the wheel. The knocking was still there behind him, in the engine in the boot, but it wasn't stopping her from moving.

'Good girl,' he said, as he reversed and swung her round.

He drove off to work, trying hard not to bring to mind the nightmare his life had transformed into, virtually overnight.

Like some ugly, indescribable pupa.

A lump of sleet splattered on the windshield in front of his face. An image of the swastika flashed inside it.

*

Like a spider. A splattered spider.

A swastika on the side of that café run by the woman with the wooden leg in Köln, a huge red flag with the white circle and black swastika inside. He was there, now, in December, thirty-two years ago, walking through a street of pulverised wood, girders, stone and brick to that café. His unit was moving through, on the way towards Sankht Vith, although he didn't know that then. Everything was kept secret.

They had all been given some free time, just the evening. And he was thinking, how could you possibly make such a mess of things?

He'd visited Köln as a young boy with his family. Whilst not particularly pious, his father loved religious architecture and would always seek out churches and monasteries on their family trips. Theo remembered hours of (mostly) endless boredom, clambering up belfries, traipsing around cold naves, his gaze being directed to carved pulpits and stained-glass windows as his father described the acts of saints, the symbols of flora and fauna. He remembered how in Köln Berne and Jürgen had decided the Cathedral was best but he, contrary as always, had pronounced his favourite to be the Romanesque church of St Kunibert, whose towers took on a fiery orange colour when lit at night.

But now, having walked past St Kunibert in Innenstadt just half an hour ago, he'd seen the western tower crushed and most of the roof collapsed. The allied bombers had destroyed it, as they had so much of the great historic town.

It made him sick. How could such work and beauty be irrevocably destroyed? For what?

This was the true destiny of the Herrenrasse, the master race.

Ashes.

The café was largely empty, just a sad series of small round tables and chairs under unflattering yellow light. No intimacy. He scanned the clientele, a couple of officers, an old man in a suit and… there, in the corner, the journalist, Sophie Fischer. His heart skipped a beat.

She was looking very elegant in a black dress with her red lipstick and hair tied up. She saw him and gestured to him with a smile.

He didn't want to go over but did. Something about her languid charm, an air of detached intelligence. And she was one of his idols. *Had been* one of his idols.

He signalled to the waiter, a bald fellow who responded in a surprisingly chipper fashion, given the situation outside.

'Schnapps,' he said. 'Would you like one?'

Sophie nodded to the waiter as Theo sat down. She was smoking a cigarette in a holder.

'Have one of these in return?' she asked, offering him her pack of Junos. He didn't want to take anything from her but he'd not had a proper cigarette in months. At the time he wasn't committed to rollies, like he was now. So he fingered one from the packet.

'The Führer doesn't approve of smoking,' she said. 'He thinks it causes lung cancer.'

'I know,' he replied.

She struck a match and he leant forward to light the cigarette. He drew in the smoke and exhaled it down to the side of the table. The way it rolled away across the tiled floor made him think of carpet bombing. Bombing a toy-sized landscape. His father, with all his painted lead soldiers, his elaborately staged war games on the shed table, would appreciate the analogy. Perhaps.

Sophie Fischer leaned forward and gazed at him with her clear green eyes.

'You look like a writer to me,' she said. Her voice was low, husky.

'No, not me,' he said. 'Not really. A few articles for the HJ, that's all.'

'That makes you a writer,' she said. 'What kind of articles?'

'Your kind of thing,' he said. 'All the *Ubermensch* stuff. Propaganda. A little more sceptical than yours, perhaps. But it was a while ago.'

'Oh yes, because you're so old,' she said, teasingly. 'But things have changed now?'

He dipped his head as the waiter reappeared, placed two glasses of Schnapps on the table.

'You don't have the fervour anymore? For the Fatherland?'

'I never had the fervour,' he said.

'You want to watch out.'

He gave a slight shrug. Once upon a time such talk could mean something. But they both knew that now, it didn't.

'You think the grand project to secure our rightful land is finished?'

He bristled and she knew it, he could see it in her eyes. Satisfaction. He drank half his Schnapps, feeling the sharpness of the alcohol change him, divert his emotion, help him stay focused, in control.

'You're going to tell me it's all about belief next,' he said.

She smiled, sat back. 'You're too intelligent for that,' she said.

'There's only one thing I want to know,' he said.

'What's that?'

'Where did you take that boy?'

'The boy? Oh, that boy,' she said. 'To the doctor, like we said. His mother was sick.'

'Mother, was it? I thought it was his father,' said Theo. 'I saw his photo on a poster. A missing persons poster.'

'It must have been someone else.'

He stared at her, saw her eyes narrow, just a little. Then he leaned forward so his nose was close to hers and said: 'I know you spent time in Wewelsburg Castle with Himmler and I read what you wrote about the Thule society. I know you're interested in the Völkisch movement, and that you're a proponent of ariosophy.'

'And…?' She smiled, holding his gaze.

'And murder is murder, no matter what the belief or circumstance.'

'Woah, that's an accusation,' she said, sitting back. 'And a very bold one at that, considering how aware you seem to be of my connections.'

'In a world full of threats, one more makes no difference,' said Theo, looking away.

'You're right,' she said, blowing smoke across the table. 'But you concentrate on your job for now, Private. We have a great deal more need of soldiers than detectives.'

*

Snow. Snow on snow. Eastbourne appearing again, its streetlights scoured by sleet on the faded plain below. Despite the blizzard, it was a reassuring scene somehow, the human glow amid the desolation, at once frail and assured. What was that line from scripture, about the light shining and the darkness not overcoming it? Still has not overcome it.

That was it. The whole condition in a nutshell. Life was the light darkness had failed to overcome. So far.

She did something unforgivable with that boy. With Dieter, he guessed, in some basement, in some Nazi pseudo-occult sacrifice to assist the war effort, or to preserve their fickle skins, or… whatever.

He knew they did.

And, in some obscure way, it had been successful. Their sick transgressive act had gained them continued existence after death.

And now they were back to ruin his life, too.

Nat

She wanted a coffee.

She hadn't eaten anything for breakfast, the thought of something touching her stomach made her feel sick. She couldn't believe it, couldn't even think of all that had happened, been said. A life reduced to nothing, in a little over forty-eight hours. *Their* lives.

Reduced to nothing.

She had seen the soldier before, of course. She remembered when he first appeared to her, all those Christmases ago, when she had been alone, like now, alone in Black Beacon, looking after her daughter. Her beautiful baby girl. Daisy. An unremarkable flower, but the one Nat loved above all, she remembered making daisy chains as a girl, the way nature produced a lovely necklace for anyone, no matter if your parents were poor as church mice, you could still make a pretty necklace for free in the garden. All you had to do was pick and splice stems, thread them into each other.

She had been sitting with her baby in front of the fire, it was the real coal fire then, not the electric one they'd replaced it with three years ago. She'd been playing with Daisy on a blanket, hiding her face behind her hands and spreading her fingers and whispering *peekaboo*, when she'd become aware of his presence, a shadow across the living room light. As she'd turned she'd felt a cold dread, a kind of suspended terror. The room had gone strange, the empty fruit bowl in the shape of a leaf gleaming and silvery, the picture of Notre Dame sharp and black, framed like something deadly on the wall.

And there he was, the German soldier, standing above them, his guts spilling out like a squid's tentacles, dots of blood all across his handsome face.

She began to hyperventilate as he lifted his open palms towards the innocent child.

The kettle began to whistle and she took it off the stove. The cup was waiting with its spoonful of Maxwell House, but she left it there and instead walked over to the table and sat down. Outside the snow was falling and she realised that it would almost certainly be a white Christmas, the thing everyone always hoped for.

But what hope was there for her?

None. There was no hope for her.

A movement at the corner of her eye made her spin in her seat, staring at the frosted window of the back door. She was sure a shadow had crossed it, even thought she'd heard the thump of a footstep on the concrete path. She couldn't take any more of this, there was a whirlpool of weakness in her body, at the centre of her mind, a place where all feeling, all spirit dissolved.

'Go away!' she screamed. She leaned forward on her elbows, bit at her nails, something she'd not done since she was a little girl.

There was a sudden clacking in the hall, tinny but insistent.

The door knocker.

Nat thought of the young woman, her beautiful daughter, grown, no, don't be stupid, not your daughter, how could it be, your daughter is dead, taken by a tumour before she was a year old, taken because of what you did…

'No…' she whispered, as the door tatted again.

She couldn't stand this. She really couldn't. Her nerves were in shreds.

Tat-tat-tat.

'Go…!' she yelled, and then felt something, the same thing she'd felt eighteen years ago, when she was playing peekaboo on the living room carpet with her daughter.

Dread.

Ice-cold dread.

She turned and they were both standing there, in the kitchen, behind her.

Theo

Things to be grateful for.

The car made it to work.

The bakery was warm and smelt good as always, of sweet bread and almonds.

And... Ray was not there in his usual seat in the canteen, sipping tea and eating a sausage roll. Theo had been dreading seeing him, the confused feelings, how would they be resolved, what was he going to do, say? Could he control his temper, the fiery temper that so often got him into trouble? What if he hit him, would he get the sack? Then what?

But... where was he?

'Sick,' said his boss, Tim Knotts, still nursing reddish bruises on both cheeks from the scrap in the pub.

'Ach,' said Theo, looking down at the table. The feeble piece of shit, he thought. Probably for the best, though. He knew at once he needed a bit of time before he saw him again. And now he'd at least have the Christmas break.

'Slice of Stollen?' said Tim.

Theo took the piece of warm fruit bread Tim proffered.

'Thought you'd like that,' said his boss. 'Did you use to eat it back home?'

Theo smiled and began to wolf it down, feeling the rawness in his stomach fade with each sweet bite.

'You look like you've had another night on the lash,' said Jeff Cooper, the newbie who knew so much about the war. There was a large, yellowish spot on the edge of his cheek.

'Yes.' Theo nodded and pushed the last mouthful of the German Christmas bread into his mouth, then stood up.

Time to get started.

Nat

She thought, as if in a dream, why do they bother knocking if they can come in anyway?

They had come and gone now and she knew what she had to do. They had told her, in unequivocal terms.

She checked that everything was off, the cooker and lights, and gave the table and units a quick wipe over with the Vim. Old habits dying hard. Then walked into the living room and got down on her hands and knees by the sofa. She peered beneath it and saw Amber lying there in the shadows. Nat reached under but could only touch her with the edge of her fingertips. She sat up and looked around. She could try and move the sofa or… she took a magazine off the table, Good Housekeeping, and rolled it up. She used that to extend her reach and push the doll out.

On her knees, Nat brushed a cobweb away from the top of Amber's face, picked a few silky threads from her golden hair. She pushed the two sides of the crack together, her thumb squeezing the rubber. No, there was no fixing it.

Nat stared into the doll's starry blue, glassy eyes.

Amber gazed back at her with frozen pupils.

Slowly, Nat shook her head. Then put the doll on the coffee table and stood up. She walked out into the hall and, taking off her house coat, lifted her long checked coat from the stand, pushed her arms through the sleeves and shuffled her shoulders to adjust it.

She reached up and turned the latch of the front door, pulled it inward.

Outside, she could see the drive, the small garden, the low brick wall with its wooden gate to the snowy downs beyond.

Schlampe, he called her. She had spent two years learning German, when they were considering a move to Kaiserslautern in the late 50s. She knew what it meant.

Schlampe. Loose woman. *Slut*.

She walked out, not closing the door.

Theo

He slid the giant spatula in and out of the oven, swiftly retrieving twelve finger buns at a time, each ready for its snow-white topping of icing.

Theo was dressed in his white apron and hat, working on his own on the oven. It suited him that way. He was thinking about it being Christmas Eve, such a big day in his life. How on this day thirty-two years ago, he had awoken, returned to himself, in a field hospital, just a giant tent really, surrounded by wounded men on tables and working men in khaki slacks, searing with pain but alive, alive under light, artificial lights suspended from canvas, cables hanging down – and he could see more light, daylight, through the canvas too, brightened by the reflection of the snow outside.

He lay there, breathing quietly, looking up, lizard-like, immobile on a slab, staring at the light. There was noise all around but it didn't penetrate his consciousness. He was something preternatural, existing because that was the way it was, that was all there was to do.

He jerked, physically jerked, when he remembered the explosion.

And then it all came pouring back in, in through his head and through his damaged body. Whiteness, the erasure of his ears with noise, the burning of his eyes by a white star. Star of wonder, star of light. Star of disintegration. So bright.

The commander, the goggles, the mounted gun, the Panzerschreck, Dieter's droning voice…

Death. He should have been dead. There had been an explosion. An explosion that he'd somehow, somehow… survived.

A miracle.

Where was Dieter?

How long had he been here?

And then, swiftly following the questions, the pain. His body raged against him, fiercest along his lefthand side. He tried to move. His right hand, right arm responded. The toes on his right foot too. He could wobble his head, but now he thought about it, the noises around him were muffled, like he was hearing through thick glass, or deep underwater. Was his hearing damaged?

He tried to sit up but couldn't. His neck was fixed, held in a brace. The skin on his face was tight.

Oh, he had survived, but how? And at what cost?

The people who were moving around, amid the wounded or dead – they were not his people. He could tell. They wore different clothes, looser, a lighter green, and they were less clean shaven. His hearing was impaired, muffled, echoey, whistling, but he could tell they weren't talking German. No, they were Americans.

He had been captured. Saved by the Americans. How?

Did they lose the battle of Sankht Vith? He had thought things were going their way. Although, of course, you could never tell in the chaotic tunnel vision of battle.

He first made the association with Christmas when one of the American surgeons passed him wearing a band of tinsel around his neck. Where had he found that?

'Hello,' Theo said, in English. His voice worked, at least.

The man stopped. He was pallid, light-haired, with a squint in his left eye.

'Holy mackerel, he talks the lingo,' said the surgeon.

'A little.'

'Well then, a Happy Christmas to you,' said the man.

'It's Christmas?'

'Near enough. Christmas Eve.'

Theo made a calculation. 'Three days,' he said.

'You've been out?' The man looked at a notepad he held on a clipboard. 'Yep,' he said. 'Three long days.'

'How… how am I…'

'Injured? I'm not going to kid you, buddy. The bad news is: terribly. But there's good news, too.'

Theo managed, he thought, a small smile. 'I'm alive,' he said.

'You got it.'

Theo was surprisingly pleased that the man didn't move on immediately, despite clearly being up to his eyeballs in it. He recognised the surgeon's deathly pallor, the greyness around his eyes, from lack of sleep. But there was something else there, a light, resilience.

'I thought we were winning,' he rasped.

'Yet more bad news for you,' said the man.

'Pardon?' said Theo. The background noise, the shouts and groans, alongside the muffling of his ears, was making it difficult to hear the man's voice.

'I said there's more bad news for you, buddy.'

'We lost?'

'Nope. You won.'

'Oh. It's bad news for all of us if we… if we Jerrys win,' said Theo, following his logic.

'That's correct. But don't worry, we're going to be taking it back. It's just a whole lot more people are gonna have to die doing it.'

'I'm…' Theo felt his eyes burning. Tears. 'Ach, I'm sorry,' he said.

The man laughed. 'Oh, that's alright, then,' he said. He looked over his shoulder to one of his colleagues. 'Guy here says he's sorry.'

The man, who was administering an injection into a boy whose eyes were closed and who scarcely looked to be in his teens, rolled his eyes.

'Do you wanna know the damage, then?' said the American.

Theo nodded, as much as he could with the neck brace.

'You have third degree burns running from your upper to lower back, around your buttocks, left leg, and left arm. You have mesenteric perforations, a punctured lung, and, bad luck, buddy, you have testicular rupture…'

'OK,' said Theo. He swallowed.

'That enough for now? I'm sure. You were saved by our friends from the Red Cross. Luckily for you, when they were retreating from the battle they saw you move. Picked you up and ferried you away in their ambulance.

These guys, they can't help themselves. So that's how you're here. Count yourself very lucky.'

Theo had no memory of being conscious after the blast.

'Do you know if my colleague survived?'

The surgeon looked around. 'There's Jonas,' he said. 'I'll check with him, I think he was there.'

Theo was surprised, humbled, by the friendliness of the man. They had been shooting bullets, calling in artillery to obliterate each other, just a few days ago. And now this. Nothing made sense, not really, did it?

Moments later, the surgeon was back.

'Sorry, buddy,' he said. 'Jonas says only you. Claims you were both mixed up like a tossed salad in the blast. The other guy didn't make it.'

Theo felt a flurry of disgust at the image of the salad. Why was that necessary?

But then, of course, they were enemies. And your enemy, well – he could only ever be so human.

*

He lost control of the spatula and a couple of buns tipped on the floor before he could turn it.

'Scheisse,' he muttered, sliding the remainder on to the icing tray then stooping and tossing the dropped ones in the bin.

Testicular rupture. Of all the things the surgeon had said to him, that was the one that whacked him round the head, made him feel sick and feeble inside. And, by turns, angry. Furious. The great leader, the Führer himself, had promised so much to the people, the youth, of Germany. And in the end it was just one great big crock of shit. The one duty any government must do above all else was protect its people. And his government had failed atrociously, catastrophically, in that one task. God, he was angry, and he had every right to be. He must have been on morphine, the other wounds ached but not insufferably – unless there was so much nerve damage he couldn't feel them? – but damage to his balls, the idea of that, ach, it was too much…

But the news had got better over the next few days. The field hospital didn't need to move, he picked up that the German advance had been stalled. A counteroffensive of a counteroffensive… Which was good. Theo had long ago realised it was only a matter of time before the Allies – and the more fearsome Soviets – defeated the Third Reich, so the sooner the better. More lives saved from this stupid, idiot war.

And his body was improving with the incredible operations they'd done on it, cutting and stitching it all back into a semblance of its former shape… he would never know how to thank them enough. He, who had tried his hardest to kill them. Them, who in return had saved his life.

He remembered that two years later he would think similar thoughts about Nat, about how the V1s he'd been involved in launching in France could have blown her to smithereens hundreds of miles away – and now they were lovers and getting married…

No, it didn't make sense. Not at all. The world was absurd.

After a few days, he was moved from the field hospital to a municipal building in another town, he didn't know which, somewhere deeper in Belgium, where he convalesced with dozens of wounded members of the Wehrmacht. There, another doctor had informed him that his hearing would return properly – although he may well suffer from tinnitus for the rest of his life – and he should also be able to *perform* again, although there might be issues with children. He'd almost cried with joy. As a young man, the ability to have sex was more important – much more important – than having offspring. He felt an overwhelming relief.

Not long after he and Nat began dating, he'd told her that his fertility might have been impaired by his injuries. He didn't want to mess her around, knew that for many women this would be a deal breaker. But Nat hadn't cared, she'd told him how much she was in love with him, and that was all that mattered. Again he was bewildered, incredulous, joyous about these people, once his enemy but with whom he now realised he shared so much. So much common decency, humanity. And love. What had it all been about, his young life?

Delusion. That was all. A trick of the mind, a mass deception. He had been a fool. Just like so many others.

With the knowledge that it may take time for Nat to become pregnant, they'd started trying from day one of their marriage. But the years of nothing began to accumulate. He had started to doubt it would ever happen, become increasingly certain of it. Yet she had not wavered in her love, in her optimism, and he had been pulled along by it.

And then, of course, eight years later, one spring morning, she had come running across the downs to find him where he was doing some fencing, a small weekend job, for Farmer Wolfson.

The miracle had happened.

The miracle he knew now was no miracle at all.

Nat

After a while, it stopped being cold.

She had been walking for what felt like hours, up over the Beacon and then down into the curved valley beyond, before ascending once again towards Beachy Head. It was hard work, the snow was getting deep in places, her thighs were sore and her feet were so heavy and numb it felt like she was lifting a sledgehammer with every step. At least the snowfall had slowed, so all she was seeing now was a sprinkle of tiny flakes, so frail they were as likely to blow back up in the sky as fall to the ground. The cloud cover was luminescent, grey, but mixed with a milky whiteness. She still could not see the sea.

It wouldn't be visible until she neared the cliff, she knew that. Because of the lie of the land.

She came to the road, waited for an old Chrysler to crawl by slowly, headlights relieving the gloom, packed with a young family. The mum, head hidden by a thick scarf and pompom hat, watched her intently. Nat feared she might turn, say something to her husband, and then they would stop. And then what, what would she say to them? But soon the red taillights had passed by and she crossed over the road, shifting and slipping a little on patches of ice.

Nat began to climb the final hill, blinking as dots of snow whisked past her lashes into her eyes.

She knew now, she had brought this on herself. The ghost, he was surely here because of Theo. He was German, after all. But what he wanted was all to do with her.

Her betrayal.

That was why he had appeared that first December of Daisy's life. He had come to take her baby away from her. The baby conceived outside of wedlock, conceived on a strange, intense afternoon at Ray Teal's house, when she'd called round on the off chance to see Lily but found him there alone instead. Lily had gone to Brighton, he explained, shopping with a friend in the Lanes. She wouldn't be back til teatime, but he invited her in anyway, gave her a tot of gin as the sun was *past the yardarm* and then…

She still could never say why it happened. Sitting together on the sofa, he'd made her giggle by telling her jokes he'd heard from a comedian the night before down the Conservative Club. Then he poured another drink, and another, and then there was a moment between them when they'd gone quiet, just looking at each other, she'd been thinking how similar in some ways he was to

Theo and before she could say something they were kissing and, well…

Daisy was not Theo's baby. No.

It had happened only once. They'd never spoken about it after. But Ray was a good friend of Theo's, he knew all about what had happened to him in the war and so… she was sure he knew it was his child. Knew when Theo asked him to be godfather, when he stood there in his blue suit in the nave, keeping his cool. Knew when he brought the doll round, telling them he realised she was too young for it now but it was intended as a present that would last, that she would grow into.

Ray knew. And he kept quiet.

But he wasn't the only one who knew.

No, somehow that desolate creature from the Other Side knew too. And he was determined to make her suffer terribly for it, first by cursing Daisy, her poor little girl, by insinuating that horrific growth into her brain, and now, when everything should be forgotten, by bringing an image, a fresh vision, of what Daisy could, *should* have been, a beautiful, fresh-faced woman with white skin and red lips and shining eyes, lighting up her life. But now Nat remembered what her mum had always talked about, her mum who believed in faeries in the garden and witches on the downs, she'd talked about the power of sprites to make a glamour – a spell that befuddled the mind and made you believe in a magical, often devastating, vision. Was that what had happened? Did they want to rub her nose in it like a dog, a dumb beast, to make her smell the foul odour of what she had done?

As if she had never known that revolting reek.

And now, at last, after all these terrifying years, he had dealt the final, crushing blow, by making Nat's eternal sin known to the one love she had left, her husband. The one person who gave her life meaning.

No, it was all over now.

She was approaching the brow of the hill, the snow-steeped land levelling off. The horizon was close, less than a hundred yards away. Her knuckles were white but she wasn't feeling the cold anymore. Her legs were tired though, shaking from the effort of trudging through the snow.

The sea came in sight. A monochrome spread dashed with white horses, a harsh scouring up to the horizon where it ended in an odd, pearly glow. It made her shudder to look at it. The very idea of coldness. She sometimes went down to see the swimmers go in on New Year's Day, down by the bandstand. How could they?

And yet…

She marched the last few yards to the edge, seeing the cliffs dropping away to either side of her, more whiteness, creamier than she'd remembered, the faint yellow of the weathered chalk revealed only by contrast to the pure white of the settled snow.

Nat came up to the place where the snow ended, felt a blast of chill air as the land fell away. She looked down through the salty swirl of the snow, down to the piled rocks and waves far below. Off to the left, she could see the red and white stripes of the lighthouse, sticking upright from the water.

Was this it?

This was it. She had failed. Her life had become failure.

She was a failure.

She lifted her foot a little over the edge, felt giddy with the thought of the fall.

It was time to fall, into the grand, yawning emptiness beyond her.

Just one small step, that was all it took.

One.

Small.

Step.

The Two Drivers

Theo

'One thing I'd really like to know is what the ordinary, everyday people thought?'

It was all he needed right now.

In the canteen, Theo had been silently eating his cheese and pickle sandwich when Jeff came and sat with him. Having reached the conclusion that, with the splitting headache from the booze, he was unable to process the events of the past forty-eight hours, he had been doing his best just to keep it together.

One small step at a time.

But there was something about the young man he warmed to so, despite Jeff's large, unpressed whitehead making him feel even queasier, he'd managed to entertain his chitchat about the pub brawl and the shenanigans of heaps of relatives coming to stay for Christmas despite the constraints of their tiny two-bed terrace. This had led Theo to remark how he'd shared a small bedroom with his brothers for the first nine years of his life – he and Berne in a bunkbed, stocky Jürgen in a camp bed – and then Jeff had asked the question about the war.

Theo paused, staring at him.

'I mean, honestly, I know people must ask you stuff like that all the time,' said Jeff hurriedly. 'Tell me to get lost if you like…'

'No one asks me anything like that.'

'Oh.' Jeff's expression dropped.

'But I don't mind,' said Theo. He pulled his baccy out his pocket and began to make a rollie. 'Most people kept their heads down. They were worried by the increasing attacks on Jews. There'd always been antisemitism. It was common, but people didn't like the new acts of vandalism, and especially the violence. But there was still a lot of people angry about the Armistice and the Nazis were at least offering some sense of renewed pride, of national unity. That went a long way to smoothing over some of the awkwardness people felt about the scapegoating of the Jews and clamp down on other freedoms.

'I was young and idealistic. The togetherness championed by the Nazis became the thing we defined ourselves around. I had a rebellious streak, I liked to challenge things, but I was always careful not to go too far.'

He looked Jeff in the eye. 'And I admit, I did get off on some of that silly mythmaking about the Aryans, even though I'm no Aryan myself. There was something exciting and pure about it, and young people want nothing more than to feel pure, to feel special and pure. Or at least I did. In fact, I reckon the Nazi ideology was really geared towards the youth. More than to adults. They were like a bunch of overgrown teenagers with a murderous streak thrown in for good measure. A publicly licensed mafia. And for a few years, I was carried away with it.

He took a match out of his Swan Vestas pack and ripped it down the strip. Lit the tip of his rollie. 'But it only took a few months of fighting to change my mind,' he added.

'I like that,' said Jeff, chuckling. 'An ideology for the kids. Makes sense.' He leaned forward. 'Did you ever kill anyone, Theo?'

Theo winced. The lad really was immune to social etiquette. But there was something OK about that, too, because Theo was no etiquette lover himself. There was something that – just a little – reminded him of himself in Jeff. The curiosity, the need to know. At least, that what he had been like as a kid. As for now...

He'd only ever talked about all this to Ray – and Nat, to a lesser extent – but that was years ago, decades, in fact. It had all been buried away, except for the odd occasion when some *dummkopf* like the guy in the pub raked it up again. (There he goes, thinking in German again, increasingly now since the accident.) But he didn't mind talking to this lad about it. Perhaps it was Jeff's enthusiasm, perhaps it was a dawning realisation that he, Theo, was one of an increasing minority who could pass on their experience of that atrocious collective failure to the next generation. His own small contribution toward trying to ensure it never happened again.

'The honest answer is, I don't know,' he said. 'I knew there were some who couldn't fire on the… enemy. They weren't cowards, they stood up alongside their brothers in the heat of battle and took the damage – it's just they couldn't bring themselves to kill.'

'Really?'

'For sure. There were lots like that. They'd run full speed into gunfire but when it came to taking aim themselves… they'd fire high, off into the air. I'd learnt that there are very few born killers, people who can take a life without destroying themselves too. But I… I certainly tried to, and I remember seeing a man fall when I shot at him across a field.

'But, at the end of the day, I suppose, I don't know…'

'When you were injured and captured – was it the Yanks who saved you?'

'The Americans. Yes.' Theo would never be able to call them *yanks*, not after what they'd done for him. He thought again about the field hospital, that kind and humorous surgeon, and then the odd thing he'd said, that had stayed with him down the years.

You were all mixed up like a tossed salad.

Like a tossed salad. Was that how…?

Despite everything, the knowledge of her betrayal, the need to be back with his wife, back with Nat again, came like a slice in his gut.

No one

In Black Beacon, the brown rotary phone on the hall table was ringing.

If someone had been there to hear it they would have noticed how the sound of the bell was a little thinner than usual, not because it was broken or obstructed in any way but because the acoustics in the hall were changed, changed by the front door being open, and by the wind and snowflakes finding their way in.

After a minute or so, on the other end of the line in a red phone box in a busy street in Lewisham, London, Tina Merrick finally set the receiver back in the cradle and waited as her coins clattered down to the refund tray.

Then she shoved open the heavy door and walked up to her husband, Terry, who was waiting for her on the street.

'No answer,' she said.

'Must be out celebrating,' said Terry.

'I don't think so.' Tina frowned, stepping back from the curb as a black cab rumbled past, a little too close, in the sleet.

Theo

Thankfully, the shift was two hours' shorter than usual, allowing them to finish early for Christmas.

Theo took out his last batch of loaves and was in the changing room and whipping off his whites ten minutes early. Bidding a hasty Merry Christmas to his colleagues, he rushed out the back of the bakery and paused, feeling the brace of the freezing air. Then he clumped through the settled snow to the Beetle, unlocked the door and clambered behind the wheel. Pulled out the choke and turned the ignition.

The good old girl started first time!

He eased her over the ridge of compacted snow that had built up along the edge of his parking space and then revved her down the road, which had been partially cleared by the passing of cars. The rear wing slid on a patch of black ice and he was lucky a burst of acceleration prevented him from clouting a parked Mini.

He slowed down, realising that, despite his increasing anxiety, he needed to take it easy or he'd have an accident. *Another* accident.

And then… then what?

*

Out of town, the old car struggled again on the road leading up to the top of the downs. Other traffic, light as it was, had managed to melt some of the snow, but there were still treacherous stretches where he worried he might lose control. At one stage, on a particularly steep incline, the car began sliding backwards causing Theo to panic and slam on the brakes. That only made the slide worse and he realised as the vehicle began to drift laterally across the road that there were two possible outcomes, either a soft bump into the bank on the left or a plunge down the open hillside to the right.

Thankfully, completely outside of his handling, the vehicle went left and nudged gently up against the bank before stopping. The daylight was good but still he switched the lights to full beam to help him navigate more carefully out of the icy patch, and be once more on his way back to Black Beacon.

Back to Nat.

*

Finally, he made it to the clump of blackthorn that preceded the narrow turn into Black Beacon's long drive. He noticed how stark, almost violent, the thorny shrubs appeared against the pure white of the snow all around. Briefly thought how strange it was, to have such a cold Christmas after the summer they'd had, with one of the longest droughts on record. It was hard to imagine himself just a few months ago lying on the lounger in the garden, fag in hand, ladybirds everywhere, wondering how much more heat he could take before retreating inside to the shade. Him, a sun worshipper with a perpetual, mahogany tan, who could spend the whole day outdoors without getting burned…

It couldn't be more opposite to this.

As soon as he stopped outside the house he swallowed hard, seeing the front door wide open. 'Aye, aye, aye…' he muttered. It felt like a hand had grabbed him around the throat. He climbed out of the car and ran inside.

'Nat!' he shouted, seeing a smattering of snow on the doormat.

'Nat, where are you?'

He ran into the living room, saw the undecorated tree in the bay, Amber with her hairline fracture lying face up, knees bent outward, on the coffee table. He darted to the dining room, swinging on the door frame to look inside, then swung back and checked the kitchen.

Empty. She wasn't there. He spotted the mug by the kettle with a spoon in it, the lid off the Maxwell House beside it.

He ran upstairs, yelling *Nat* all the way.

Moments later, he was back down, certain she wasn't in the house. He felt suddenly, unnervingly, short of breath, a moment of sheer panic that he wouldn't be able to breathe. He heard a faint whistling, his lungs struggling to draw in air.

He reached his hand towards the wall, managing to knock the picture of Geronimo off. It fell heavily on its frame, the glass cracking. He propped himself up, ignoring the picture, breathing heavily.

Where was she? Where had she gone?

He was sweating and an image of that storeroom in Caen came back, the rust-coloured box saying *Savon*

Dentifrice Colgate on the shelf at eye level, the box he noticed as he thrust himself up against the wall, somehow surviving the pummel of bullets from that Sten gun, how, how had he survived…?

How would he survive now, if Nat had left him? Why would she, when it was her who had betrayed him? Unless…

Unless there was something still between her and Ray.

Raking his hair, he looked out of the door, towards the snowy downs.

And saw the footprints.

'God almighty,' he said, running out into the drive. The gate in the fence was open. She had gone out on to the field. He scanned the rising slope of snow, shaded here and there by clumps of shrub and small hollows in the ground.

Nothing.

She was nowhere to be seen. Where had she gone?

An unholy gravity was pulling his thoughts and emotions one way. Towards a conclusion he knew he could never entertain.

'Nat!' he yelled, his cry muffled by the snow-packed landscape.

'Nat!'

The footsteps were smudged, blown over in places, but he could trace their trajectory off across the hill, towards the horizon.

Seaward.

Coughing, Theo began to run.

*

She had left the door open, he kept thinking, as the heat built in his limbs and he began to sweat. His lungs felt like they were being dug at by dozens of needles. He paused at the brow of the hill, clutching his knees, breath misting, staring into the valley with the winding road below.

He scanned it quickly, saw no movement anywhere in the scene before him. Just a bleak, frozen, winter's valley. Hostile, forbidding to life, sealing even the green grass away in a bright, smothering tomb of white.

'Ach,' he said, forcing himself back into a jog, wishing to God he'd never smoked a fag in his life, that he'd continued playing football with the work team… Anything to have kept himself healthy, to prevent himself feeling so much like a geriatric.

She would never leave the door open.

He ran down into the valley, snow spraying around his calves.

*

He felt his mouth drying, his throat constricting as he lolloped on to the empty, frozen road and then found himself flat on his back, wincing with pain.

He had slipped on ice and taken a nasty bang. He lay on his back, staring up at the featureless sky. Blinked, as an ice-cold flake touched his eye.

'Aye, aye, aye…' he said, twisting and easing himself up with his hands on the icy road. The big muscle in his backside hurt, he was going to have a nice bruise – another nice bruise – but he was OK. Everything was still working. He climbed back on to his feet, moved carefully over the remainder of the road, and began to ascend towards Beachy Head, panting all the way.

The footprints were much shallower now, more diced and blown over by the wind – but there were enough patches sheltered by clumps of grass and depressions for him to see where she'd been heading. Although a larger part of him was starting to wish he was wrong, that he'd been following somebody else's footprints altogether, as he knew now where they were going, knew the dark resonance of the Seven Sisters cliffs, the sinister place they held in everyone's imagination despite their rugged beauty.

Not Nat, surely, not his Nat…

*

As he stumbled towards the top of the hill, the wind grew stronger, blowing settled snow crystals up into his face. He tugged his collar against it, squinting into the increasing murk. The day was starting to fade now. Only his movement, the sting of the snow, was keeping him going, preventing him from collapsing with exhaustion, from the pain in his back and buttock, from a debilitating mix of panic and despair.

He slowed, some sort of physical, counteracting force pushing against him, contracting the muscles in his legs. For a second he thought no, he really couldn't go on, he didn't want to go on, because what if…

What if the worst thing imaginable turned out to be true?

In the dismal gloom the sea came into view, caustic and greeny-brown, barren of life and hope. An oppressive band of purplish cloud limned the horizon, the colour of an old wound. He was close to the edge, wondering what he would do when he saw the last footstep, but no, he realised now he'd lost track of the footsteps, hadn't seen one for a dozen yards or so, he'd just been stumbling on in their general direction, so perhaps he'd got it wrong, maybe she turned and headed west along the cliffs, walking, walking where…?

Wasn't there a church that way, a little isolated Norman church sitting in the next valley? Maybe she had gone there, seeking sanctuary, a place that could offer a glimmer of solace? Yes, that must be it, she'd been feeling down, very despondent after last night, perhaps even had considered doing something terrible, but then, as she made her way towards the cliff, the reality of her situation had come back to her, she'd remembered their love, knew that whilst he was upset he would always love her, love his Nat, and she'd changed her mind, perhaps realising then it was too hard, too bitter, to go all the way back to Black Beacon, no, and then she'd thought about the church, a place to get shelter from this dreadful wind and bleakness, a place where she could be safe…

'Idiot!' he shouted, dropping to his knees in anger and weakness. He had to stop this creating, like a desperate child. Sometimes you couldn't look away. Not from the man shot across a field, from the child stolen from his parents…

You had to turn and face the true nature of things.

He stood up, stumbled a little sideways, his legs aching and wobbly. He had to get to the edge. He had to steal himself to look over, look down, aware that, even if the worst possible thing had happened, he was still, well…

He couldn't even think it.

He was still unlikely to see her… down there.

'Please God,' he whispered, noticing two more prints in the snow.

He pushed himself forward, upward, towards the brow of the land, towards the place it ended. Towards the cliff.

Then noticed a few yards up, right beside the edge, a hunched shape in the snow.

Nat

She couldn't do it. She couldn't jump. She loved him too much, and she was too much of a coward.

But it had suddenly felt so very cold, the sea churning hundreds of feet below, the sweeping, ghostly fields behind. She felt so cold.

So she had laid down there, quietly, and waited.

Waited for him to come.

Theo

His euphoria faded as he drew near to her. He felt his stomach wrench.

'Nat!' he cried, falling on his knees in the snow, pulling her up by the shoulders. Her eyes fluttered open, blinking against the snow-reflected light, closing again.

'Nat…' He hugged her to him, rubbed her back, trying to make her warm. God, it was like that in the Ardennes, always the fear, out all day, sometimes all night, that the hypothermia might take hold.

'Nat, my darling, my love,' he whispered, pressing her cheek against his.

'Theo,' she said quietly. 'Knew you'd come, love…'

Her skin was deathly pale, almost transparent, sickly. He kissed her and the corner of her lips kinked with a smile. Then she closed her eyes again.

'I'm so sorry,' she said. 'Your friends…'

'You don't need to be sorry about anything,' he said. 'I love you and we're going to get you back to Black Beacon right now.'

But as he stood, lifting her under the arms, her knees straightening but not quite locking, he realised what a challenge that was going to be. Everything around was hostile. The deep snow, wind, the subdued roar of the sea below. He started by dragging her away from the treacherous edge.

'Come on, Nat,' he said. 'Walk with me...'

She managed a step but then her knee folded and she fell like a dead weight against his shoulder. He struggled to keep her upright, prevent her collapsing back in the snow. How was he going to do this?

'One step at a time,' he said. 'We'll be back in Black Beacon, we'll get the fire going, get the lights on the tree, you'll be right as rain in no time...'

'My hero,' she said.

She had never said that before. All she'd ever called him was a *right blinking hero*, one of their affectionate in-jokes. He'd only ever thought of himself as an anti-hero, on the wrong side of history, of humanity. One of the enemy, the genocidal killers. He thought of the conversation he'd had earlier with Jeff in the canteen, remembered in a flash a sublime feeling of ecstasy from his youth, experienced somewhere in the Black Forest, sun filtering through tall pines. The sublime elect...

Sublime, *murderous* elect.

He shook his head. He could do this. He could.

'Come on, duck,' he said. 'I've got you.'

He took a step forward in the snow, felt the numbness of his foot, the cold and wet soaked through.

A sudden knifing pain in his lower back. She came with him.

'One more,' he said.

'Oh,' she said into his ear, 'it's just like… las.'

He didn't hear, her voice was so strained.

'What was that, love?'

'It's just… like… like the carol… King Wenceslas…'

He smiled. 'Let's sing it,' he said and, just as he was about to start, he saw a light at the far end of the valley.

It took a moment for him to understand. The light coming through the gloom, shining out of the darkness.

'Car,' he said. 'It's a car!'

He tried to pull her along with him but realised he would miss it if he took her with him.

'Wait here, love,' he said. 'You'll be alright. I'll be back in a minute with help.'

She looked so frail in the crushed snow as he lay her down on her back. She tried to put out an arm to stay upright but quickly slipped back into the snow. Theo frowned, panicking that she might go into a worse state if he left her. But he couldn't risk losing the car, it was their only hope.

He pulled off his sheepskin coat, wrapped it as best he could around her, pulling the collar up around her face so just her eyes were peeking out.

'I'll be back soon!' he shouted and ran down the hill towards the road.

*

There were actually two cars coming carefully along the icy road, an orange Cortina and an Austin Maxi a short way behind. He wondered if they might be together.

Theo lunged into the road, wondering how he must appear, some kind of madman in a thin jumper, waving his arms over his head. He squinted against the glare of the headlights.

The car came to a halt and he shuffled towards it, slipping on the ice again, only just managing to stay on his feet.

'Can you help me?' he shouted. 'I need help!'

There was a man at the wheel, burly, a black woollen hat pulled down over his eyebrows, a woman in a beige coat beside him. The man looked shocked, possibly angry. Through the windshield, Theo could see him speaking, watching Theo, not looking at his wife. Then, as Theo came up to the side of the car, expecting him to wind down the window, there was a surge of revs and the car swung over to the other side of the road and began to drive away.

'Hey!' shouted Theo. 'Wait!'

But the car was off, he watched the taillights as it accelerated away up the hill.

Panicking, Theo turned towards the next car, the Austin Maxi, which now lit him up in its lights. Theo made an exaggerated shrug towards the disappearing Cortina, then waved his arms again at the car as it approached.

'Please stop,' he said.

The Maxi slowed and halted a few yards in front of him. This time the lone driver, a young man also wearing a black knitted hat, opened his door and stepped out.

'Are you alright, mate?' he said.

'I need some help,' said Theo. 'My wife and I went for a walk in the snow but she's got very cold and tired. I need to get her back home…'

The man looked after the disappearing Cortina. 'No help from him,' he said. 'What a bastard, driving off like that…'

'Yes,' said Theo, realising his teeth were starting to chatter. 'Will you help us?'

'Where is she?' said the man, looking up the wrong side of the hill.

'Over there,' said Theo, pointing her out above them.

'Yes, mate, of course I will,' said the man. 'What were you doing, going for a walk in this weather?'

*

The man helped Theo support Nat back to the car. Theo climbed in the back with her. She had been quite unresponsive as they brought her down the hill, murmuring to herself, but in the car she said: 'Thank you,' to the man, as he restarted the engine.

'No problems,' he said. He had a brown moustache, a little too big for his sallow face. 'Shall we take her to the hospital?' he said, looking at Theo. 'Have her checked out?'

'What do you think, love?' he said. 'Do you want to go to the hospital?'

'No,' she said. 'Just take me home.'

'There's a blanket down behind that seat, by your legs,' said the man. 'Sorry, it's the dog's – but you can use it to keep her warm.'

'Thank you,' said Theo.

As he wrapped it around her he noticed how much she was shivering.

*

A short while later they drew up in front of Black Beacon. The afternoon light was nearly gone now and a few wispy snowflakes were again starting to fall.

The man came round and opened the door, helped Theo lift Nat out from the back. Theo had managed to keep her awake all the way home, scared she might fall unconscious.

'You are so kind,' she said to the man, as they took her to the door. 'What's your name?'

'Jim,' he said.

'Thank you, Jim,' she said. 'You're a good boy.'

'Blimey, your door's open!' he said.

'Shit,' said Theo. 'We need to get that bloody latch fixed, it keeps sticking. Wind must have blown it open. One of these days we're going to get burgled!'

The young man seemed to accept the explanation as they supported Nat through into the living room and lay her down on the sofa.

'Is there anything else I can do?' said Jim as Theo led him back out into the hall.

'No, you've been a real saviour,' Theo replied. He fished in his pocket and found his wallet.

'No, mate, honestly,' said the young man, as Theo pulled out a couple of pound notes.

'I want you to have it,' said Theo.

'It's Christmas, mate.'

'Please – take it. Get yourself a bottle of something nice.'

The man smiled, took the notes and pushed them in his jeans pocket.

'Well, if there's nothing else, I'd better be on my way. The missus'll be wondering where I've got to!'

'Thank you,' said Theo as the man went out and got into his car. He watched the lights go on and the engine kick easily into life. Jim gave a small wave at the wheel, and drove away up the icy drive.

Christmas

Theo

He made her warm.

He put the heating on, turned it up full, brought some dry clothes and her dressing gown down and helped her change into them, rubbing her dry first with a towel. He moved the coffee table out of the way, put Amber on a shelf in the alcove, and lifted the comfy armchair in front of the electric fire. He eased her down into the chair, filling the gaps between her frail body and the arms with cushions and then tucking their thickest woollen blanket around her. He went out to the kitchen and made her a cup of tea with four sugars, two more than normal, put the rest of the water into a hot water bottle and brought them back to her, a packet of Digestives under his arm.

She was still shivering when he set the tea and biscuits down on the table beside her. Which he knew, from his time in Belgium, was a good thing. People with hypothermia didn't shiver.

'Come on, love,' he said. 'You're safe now.'

She smiled weakly at him in the soft light of the sidelamps. He hadn't turned on the overhead light, he thought it made the room feel colder somehow. He went over and drew the curtains against the snow-swirling night.

'It's Christmas Eve,' she said.

'That's right, duck,' he said. 'Drink your tea, it'll make you feel better.'

She took the mug in her hands and held it there.

Theo stood for a moment before a thought occurred to him. 'We haven't decorated the tree,' he said. 'I'll do it now.'

'I saw you'd got those decorations,' she said. 'I was meaning to put them up but then your friends…'

Theo stopped. She'd said that before, when he found her in the snow. Which friends? Who did she mean?

He realised then how cold he was, still in his damp clothes.

'I'd better get changed myself, first, love,' he said. 'I'll do them when I come back down.'

Nat

She stared at the three bars of the fire, such a pure, intense orange, fringed with yellow. When she looked at those bright bars, she used to imagine sometimes that the soul might look something like that. All orange and gold, pulsing light and heat.

Sometimes.

She was still cold, her teeth tapping involuntarily, but she was comforted now by the idea of warmth, its promise. A sip of hot tea and a hug of the water bottle under the blanket. She moved her toes in her slippers but was unable to give them a proper wriggle. They were still ice blocks.

He was doing such a good job. Her Theo. And she knew she didn't deserve it.

She looked across at the undecorated tree, the curtains drawn behind it.

Them.

They were still there, out in the cold. Perhaps just on the other side of those curtains, staring at the windows. Waiting to come back, to accuse her again.

Why hadn't she done it? Why didn't she jump?

Why would she never leave Theo alone?

He deserved better than her. Only by getting out of his life – permanently – would she ever let him be free.

She turned back to the fire and sniffed, as a tear ran down her cheek.

Theo

He was back again with the Co-op bag full of decorations.

'I'll put the lights on first,' he said.

'Let me help you,' she said.

'Don't be silly. You stay there.'

He got into a right old mess, though, tangling the wire. And then she was there, beside him, holding the lights out with spread arms so it was easier for him to thread them through the branches.

'You're alright?' he said.

'Better,' she said.

He placed the last strand of the lights at the base of the leader, the highest branch rising straight from the trunk.

'You sit down again, duck,' he said. 'I'll finish it off.'

'Alright.'

He watched her as she moved stiltedly back to the chair, sat down heavily and tugged the blanket over her knees. Then he turned his attention back to the tree. He had two boxes of baubles, one red set and the other silver. He picked them out carefully, fiddling with the looped threads and muttering as he tried to hoop them over the needles. But eventually he had them arranged around the tree and he finished it off with the gold star on the top.

'Go on, switch it on,' said Nat.

He did and they both gazed in wonder at the starry lights, some bright, others obscured, all magical.

Theo checked his wristwatch. It was a quarter past eight.

'Do you want me to make you something to eat?' he said.

'I'll stick with the biscuits for now. Maybe some cheese and crackers later. For supper.'

His every muscle hurt but strangely his headache had gone. 'Fancy a small whiskey? It might help us warm up.'

She nodded and he came back with the half bottle and two tumblers. He set them down on the coffee table and moved the other chair, Amber's chair, alongside her.

'Oh, I know,' he said, and walked over to the hifi.

'What are you putting on?'

'Wait and see.'

He removed an LP from the shelf, slid it out of its sleeve.

'Oh yes, that one,' she said, with a smile.

He put the record on the turntable, then lowered the needle down. After several seconds of hushed crackling, the choir began to sing:

Stille nacht, Heilige nacht, Alles schläft, Einsam wacht...

'Your favourite,' she said, as he sat down beside her.

He poured them whiskey.

'Merry Christmas,' he said, toasting her.

She raised her glass to his. 'It's not Christmas yet.'

'Very nearly,' he said.

Nat

She opened her eyes and looked at the fire, bright and precious, in front of her.

Wriggled her toes, properly warm now. She'd thought they were never going to feel warm again.

The music, the German carols, had stopped, she noticed. The tumbler of whiskey was still in her hand. She wondered if she had dozed off, everything felt fuzzy and warm and safe...

Theo. He had come for her. He was back. Sitting beside her. She turned to look at him.

He was there, asleep in the armchair, cheek against his shoulder.

The soldier with the spilling guts beside him.

Theo

'Nat, Nat!'

He held her shoulders, pushed her back, trying to stop her shuddering, gasping.

'You've been asleep, Nat – you fell asleep!'

She opened her eyes wide, staring quickly left and right, then looking hard back over each shoulder. Pinching her lips with her fingers.

'He was here – here again…' she said.

'You were dreaming, Nat,' he said. 'A nightmare. But you're safe, I'm here.'

'Your friend, he was there, right behind you, behind the chair…'

'He's not my friend, love. He was never my friend.'

She looked up at him, into his dark, steady eyes. His hair, pushed out of shape in his sleep, stood high above his head, like the wavy, Brylcreemed style he'd had when she first met him. Or like some glam rocker, David Bowie or that guy from Sweet…

'Why did you say that?' he asked.

'What?' she said.

'That he's my friend – that the ghost is my friend?'

She felt her face crumpling, the resurgence of guilt. 'Because… because he first came when I… when I betrayed you…'

'What do you mean?'

'The first time I saw him… it was when she was born. I should have told you then! When our little… when Daisy was born… Oh love, I'm sorry, I'm so sorry…'

'Stop saying that, Nat. I forgive you.' And he knew then that he did, he really did. Daisy's death had been as traumatic for him as it was for her, if not more so, but the pain – it had become manageable after a few years. A weakness, spiritual soreness, that he had learned to live with. So now, when he found out that she hadn't been his child – his *natural* child – he was surprised that it didn't feel like the end of the world. And he still loved that baby – with all his heart.

And Nat's betrayal with Ray… that hurt, of course, like a dagger inside, but it was a long time ago and he… well, he knew she meant more to him than that. Much, much more. He knew from the moment he'd realised she'd gone missing on the downs how much more. Sex was sex but love… love was all that mattered.

And he loved Nat, more than anything else he could imagine.

'These things happen,' he said. 'I couldn't give you a child. You wanted a child. These things… they happen…'

She cried. He leaned forward, awkwardly, puts his arms around her neck as she sobbed.

'There, there, love,' he said. 'I'm sorry too, that I never properly discussed it with you, when you mentioned the ghost all those years ago. I just… something was blocking it. I don't know what…'

'I'm so sorry,' she repeated, as if she hadn't heard his own apology. He let her say it. For a moment, he thought about Ray, too. It would take him time to forgive his friend, he knew that. But ultimately, he loved him too. It was nearly twenty years ago. But he wasn't going to be letting him off the hook too easily, mind…

As Nat's sobs subsided he released her from his embrace, kissed her, then sat down again. He rolled himself a cigarette, lit it by holding it against the fire rings when he found his matchbox empty.

'That man was not my friend,' he said again, blowing out smoke.

'But he came to make me suffer, because I committed a sin. He wanted to avenge you, to protect you…'

'Bullshit.'

She looked at him, surprised. He didn't use that word.

'He was Nazi scum. An occultist. There were quite a few of them around. I always hated him. He did something very… evil, pure evil… with that woman. The one you thought was Daisy, all grown up. I met them together, one night when I was in Köln, and they had a lost child with them, a boy.'

'Oh …' said Nat, frowning, anticipating the worst.

'They killed him, I'm sure, I suspect it was some kind of ritual. There were missing person notices all over town afterwards, the lad's family was rich, I imagine. I'm guessing, of course I am, Nat, but my best guess is that they did it as some kind of… supernatural *insurance*. And, perhaps because of that, when Dieter and I were blown up together, something happened…'

'What?' Nat's mouth hung open, one hand on her cheek.

'I don't know. The American surgeon said something, I remembered it earlier. He said… he said we were mixed up like a tossed salad.'

'That's horrible. What a horrible thing to say.'

'I know. But I reckon somehow, that explosion attached him… his spirit to me. Bound us together in some way. Him dead, me alive.'

'What a terrible thought…'

'And her too,' Theo continued. 'I suspect what they did, the ritual with the boy, that might have linked her spirit to his. So when she died, wherever, however she died, before or after the war, I don't know… she became part of him. Because she'd killed the boy with him.'

'How can you know any of this?'

'I don't. It's probably a load of old rubbish. But it's the only thing I can think of.'

'Theo, love, it's all so…' Nat lost her words.

He shrugged. 'It doesn't need to make sense,' he said. He took another puff on his fag, tipped himself another shot of whiskey.

Nat was thinking. 'So why was it me who saw them first?' she said.

'Because you're more sensitive than me. Like your mum was.' He remembered the shape in the forest, when he was cutting the tree. 'I've always seen shadows, glimpsed figures, but I've dismissed them. It was only after the car accident, the bang on the head, that I began to see him – and later her – clearly. Like you do. I saw someone – something – in the wood the other night when…' Bizarrely, he still didn't like to admit that he stole the tree to her. 'There was a shape, an outline, in the dark. Like someone standing there, watching me. I think it must have been him. The bastard got me lost.'

Nat reached across and gripped his hand. He took a drag on his rollie, thinking. Time to admit it, it was such a small misdemeanour in the scheme of things.

'Thinking about it, they only turn up when I – and yes, maybe you too – do something wrong. Not every time, but often. And it doesn't need to be big. Like me stealing that tree and the baubles, or drinking and driving, or getting in a fight. And maybe your... thing... with Ray let them in, too...'

'You stole the tree and baubles?'

He nodded. 'Things are tight for us this year, aren't they, love? With the mortgage and now the TV broken. But I wanted us to have a nice Christmas together. The baubles I took, just because of how they treated you in Stanley's.'

'I need some more of that,' said Nat, and poured herself a dribble of whiskey. 'And yes, they were a right bloody pair of pompous so-and-sos,' she said.

Theo's eyes brightened when he saw her chuckle.

'But Theo,' she said, after a while, 'if those... ghouls... aren't here to make me pay for what I did... what are they here for?'

Theo grimaced, staring at the fire. 'Those evil bastards just want me to suffer,' he said. 'Look at me. I've made my home, made peace, with the enemy. Married one of them, even. I betrayed everything they believed in. Everything. The *Herrenrasse*, the whole idea of the Master Race…'

He turned sharply to Nat, who was gazing at him, eyes wide.

'They hate me, duck,' he said. 'Simple as that. They're stuck in Germany, 1944, and they hate everything I stand for. They only used you to get at me. If you were unconfident, guilty, that was good for them, they could use it to undermine us, our relationship. Eventually, with their attempt today, they tried to take you away from me. To take away my most precious relationship – the reason I'm happy, why I'm… alive.'

'But Daisy… when I first saw him, he pointed at her. He…' she shook. 'He put that tumour inside her head!'

'Bullshit.'

She stared at him again.

'I don't believe that for one moment. I don't believe he has any power like that at all. The only power he has is fear, suggestion – uncertainty. Because he's dead. And dead… dead is weak. Daisy… Daisy, I'm afraid, my love… she would have died anyway.'

'It's all too much,' she whispered. Then worriedly: 'How can we know?'

Theo took a last puff on his rollie and dropped it in the ashtray. He looked at his watch.

'No,' he said. 'It's not too much. We know them now. We know what they want. And so we know not to give it to them. If they come, we will not see them. We will not. From now on – you and I – we're free. Free of their sickness. Free to live our own lives.'

She stared at him. Imagined, briefly, the ghosts, the soldier and the bright young woman, both outside on the downs, standing side by side in the snow, watching the little house with its muted Christmas lights. Watching Black Beacon. Then she picked up her tumbler and drank the whiskey.

She looked back at her husband, the man who had single-handedly lifted up her life.

'You shouldn't have stolen the tree,' she said slyly.

With the door shut, it was properly toasty in the room now. Theo smiled as he unbuttoned his cuff and rolled up his sleeve. She saw his angel tattoo as he twisted his wrist to her, showing her the time.

12:20.

'It's Christmas,' she said.

'Yes, duck,' he said. 'We're going to have a good one this year. Just look at that tree.'

She looked at the tree, looked into its heart, at the yellow lights shimmering amid the dark pine needles.

'It's beautiful,' she said at last.

Nat

There was a brightness at the curtains when she woke the next morning.

It mimicked the lightness in her head, which she first attributed to the whiskey, a bit of a hangover, but then realised was probably more to do with not having woken up once in the night for the first time in… years.

She had slept through. And it was Christmas Day!

She stretched languidly, wriggled her toes, yawned. Theo was snoring in his pyjamas beside her. She turned and looked over at the alarm clock and saw it was nearly ten o'clock. Good grief! Not only had she not woken all night, she'd slept the longest she'd slept since… well, since she couldn't remember when.

Not wanting to wake Theo, she lifted the covers carefully and pushed her feet into her slippers. She went over to the door and lifted her dressing gown off the hook, slid her arms through the sleeves. Then headed to the bathroom.

The door was ajar and she stopped at the threshold, remembering.

Remembering.

*

When she went back to the bedroom, carrying a small bag with the wrapped presents she'd bought for Theo – a new lighter, a fancy Zippo, to save him always running out of matches, a red cravat to replace the one he'd lost, and a box of Quality Street, which he always liked at Christmas – she found he'd turned over on to her side of the bed and was still snoring away. She watched the side of his face for a while, studying the rich, almost woody hue of his cheek, the sprouting black stubble – he must have missed his shave yesterday – and the dark mop of his hair, a few strands of grey showing where it had been pushed out of shape by the pillow. His lips were open a little and his snoring lessened as she stared, becoming a gentler soughing of air through his jowls. It wasn't his best look – not by any means – but it was all she could do not to grab those cheeks and plant a kiss on his pale mouth.

She turned away, put on her tights, frock and jumper, and went downstairs to make herself a cup of tea.

She took it in the living room, put another LP of carols on the stereo – quickly turning the volume down when it came on at full blast, they'd been enjoying it so much last night! – and then switched on the fire and tree lights. She turned the armchair – Amber's armchair, *their* armchair – around, so she could watch the tree as she sipped the refreshing tea.

It was lovely sitting there, in the peace of Christmas Day morning.

Lovely.

I saw three ships come sailing in, on Christmas Day, on Christmas Day, I saw three ships come sailing in, on Christmas Day in the morning…

Flakes were falling outside the bay windows. She thought about that poem by Louis MacNeice, the one her mother used to recite by heart – *Snow*. It was like that now, all she needed was the roses.

And so, here it was, snow, on Christmas Day. The ever-hoped-for snow.

When she'd finished her tea she thought she would go out and have a look at it. She went in the hall and put on her overcoat. Noticed the picture of Geronimo was still on the floor, with a crack in the glass. She put it back up on its nail, the crack wasn't terrible, after all, it would do until they could afford to replace it – then opened the front door.

The fresh cold air was something. It made the breath catch in her chest.

But the beauty was astonishing. The sky was cloudy but bright, suffused with a silvery underlay. Millions of white flakes, mishappen, grizzled, delicate, were dropping, sticking to everything, covering the car, the gate, fence, freshening yesterday's dirty snow on the fields.

Snow, snow falling on snow, snow on snow…

What magic, she thought.

And then, over there, near the patch of blackthorn, by the old dewpond – was that a movement?

She looked, heart feathery in her chest, throat tight.

No.

There was no one there – *nothing* there. No movement at all.

And then she realised: she didn't care if there was.

The ghost – ghosts – were terrifying, that was certain. But the power they held over her, particularly the power *he* held over her, him, the soldier, the bloodied one – it was all to do with Daisy. The sin of her betrayal, the deep, painful secret she'd held close, daily, in her wounded heart.

And now, just like that, Theo had forgiven her. He had let it go. So she, too, could let it go.

She breathed in the cold air and coughed.

There was no one there.

Over thirty years ago, all those brave young men and women had defeated that hellish evil, that scourge of humanity. They had gone off righteous, anxious, joyous, secretly terrified – and almost all suffered unimaginably. And now, she and Theo, they had done it again. She wasn't a philosophical person, but she had a thought that struck her as quite profound.

They were not alone. Everyone, everywhere, in the whole wide world, was defeating that evil every single day of their lives. Not just from outside, from the invasions and suppressions of governments, but in their own hearts and minds as well. And, tragically, Nat could see it was a battle that would go on forever, that would never be won. But, provided they kept at it, kept on their guard, kept fighting every day – some days easier than others, some harder – nor would it ever be lost.

The light shines in the darkness, and the darkness has not overcome it.

They did not hold power over her anymore.

With a smile – it was Christmas Day, after all, and it was snowing – Nat turned and went back inside Black Beacon.

It was time to go and wake him up, and open the presents.

Thank you for reading my book, I hope you enjoyed it!

If you did, I would be very grateful if you could post a rating or short review on Amazon or Goodreads. Your ratings make a real difference to authors, helping the books you enjoy reach more people.

Afterword

First, a minor atonement. Whilst those of us who can remember the only white Christmas of the nineteen-seventies in Eastbourne (1970) are increasingly feeling our age, I must apologise to the eagle-eyed for adding a second later in the decade. Whilst 1976 had snow in December and January and a very cold Christmas, it was not in fact white. I did this to add character to the setting, and because I wanted to write a story that was set in what was arguably the heyday of the Christmas single, when the wonderful garishness of the mid-1970s Christmases would contrast sharply with Nat and Theo's harrowing visitation.

And second, a longer note on how I came to write *Black Beacon*, which, although in many places a dark novel, is inspired by the light.

Theo and Nat are very much fictional characters with their own qualities and flaws (I'm thinking particularly of larceny and affairs) but they are inspired by real people, my grandparents, Egon and Pamela Korn. It is to their memory that I dedicate *Black Beacon*.

Here are some of the ways in which their real-life story overlapped with Theo and Nat's.

My grandfather ('Da') was from Kaiserslautern in Germany. He was conscripted as a seventeen-year-old to fight Hitler's war. He was sent first to France where, amongst other things, he had a fight with an officer that led to him being briefly imprisoned; he worked as a journalist; and he was at the launch of one of the first V1 rockets, which came back down and struck the launch site.

Most significantly, like his brothers on the African and Russian fronts, he was captured and survived as a Prisoner of War. He was injured in an incident almost identical to Theo's, the only difference being that he was at the battle of Caen after the Normandy landings, and the tank that fired on him was British. I changed the time and location to snowy St Vith to resonate with the Christmas theme of the book.

Da was rescued by the Red Cross. He was scarred all down one side from the explosion – I saw those scars (as well as the angel tattoo). He was sent as a PoW to Canada, where he told me bears looted the bins every night, then to Scotland, and finally to Eastbourne. That's where he took a young Pamela Guy to the cinema in a town at which only a year or two back he may well have been firing rockets.

What a strange way to start your adult life.

I know my grandmother, Pamela ('Nan'), and Da lived life to the full and loved each other very much. And I loved them both very much. As a boy, the height of excitement was when they turned up at our house in Kenilworth for a holiday visit, or when we went down to stay with them in Eastbourne – especially at Christmas.

Da died in 1977 when I was ten. He died of lung cancer, having had his fair share of trauma and having smoked all his life. Nan lived a lot longer, passing away in 2014. She had a couple of relationships, but never married again. She did however do some amazing things with her life. Her passions included writing, painting (particularly abstract art), religion, and Russia – she got a degree in Russian late in life, and in the year before she died was still happily beavering away translating *Dr Zhivago*. She travelled to Russia several times and came back with fabulous stories such as drinking vodka in a bar in a perpetually dark Murmansk with Russian sailors.

Above all, she was dedicated to peace. When she was a child the world was still convalescing from the first world war. Whilst she was offered the chance to evacuate, she chose not to leave Eastbourne during the very real threat of invasion at the start of the second world war, and she witnessed the heavy bombardment of the town. She then met and married my grandfather, which took some courage in itself as life would not be easy married to a former PoW. She went to live with him in Germany in the early 1950s. Being married to a German PoW and seeing the plight of mothers on both sides who'd lost sons, led her to reject violence and war in all its manifestations. She became a lifelong member of the CND and camped with the women at Greenham Common.

I'd like to finish on a poem of hers. She had poetry published and had just started working on her first novel, which isn't bad for someone in her eighties. The poem I've chosen is short but captures one of her final passions, which lasted throughout her life – her love for Eastbourne and its mesmerising downs:

MEMORIES

I close my eyes and see
green undulating downs
and smell sweet scent
of yellow cowslips.

I see round eyes of dew ponds
and remember jam jars
filled with tadpoles.

And with inward vision
see blue carpets of high-summer
nodding scabious and rampion
and hear the ticking sound
of grass-hoppers –

the memories of childhood.

And finally, *Black Beacon* is written in praise of Nan and Da's daughter, who is thankfully living a long and happy life – my wonderful mum, Lis!

Nan and Da are still with me, often in my thoughts. They show that ghosts do exist, as memory, as shapes and feelings and moments in our heads. And that ghosts are not necessarily the things of desolation we frequently imagine; they can be creatures of good, which sustain the living.

Other Books by Steve Griffin

The Ghosts of Alice

The Ghosts of Alice is a series of standalone ghost stories featuring Alice Deaton, a young woman with a mysterious connection to the dead.

The Boy in the Burgundy Hood

** THE #1 INTERNATIONAL BESTSELLER **

Will it be her dream job – or a waking nightmare?

Alice can't believe her luck when she lands a new post at a medieval English manor house. Mired in debt, the elderly owners have transferred their beloved Bramley to a heritage trust. Alice must prepare it for opening to the public, with the former owners relegated to a private wing.

But when the ghosts start appearing – the woman with the wounded hand and the boy in the burgundy hood –

Alice realises why her predecessor might have left the isolated house so soon.

As she peels back the layers of the mystery, the secrets Alice uncovers haunting Bramley's heart will be dark – darker than she could ever have imagined…

What readers say about *The Boy in the Burgundy Hood*:

***** 'The perfect modern day ghost story with a grisly twist'
***** 'Impossible to put down'
***** 'Creepy and satisfying'
***** 'A compelling and spinetingling read'
***** 'Too scared to sleep… I read it in one day!'
***** 'Turn the screw it does, right up to its terrifyingly dark finale.'

Also in *The Ghosts of Alice* series:

The Girl in the Ivory Dress

Will a strange request help her move on from a haunted past?

After a fire tears through the country house where she works, Alice accepts a desperate invitation from a friend whose guest house is being haunted.

But when Alice arrives at the remote Peacehaven, she senses something much stranger going on. Who is the ghastly spectre roaming the house? Why is he terrifying the guests? And why does Alice keep dreaming about the ghosts of her past, the burning man and girl in the ivory dress?

As she digs deeper, Alice will uncover an insidious evil that might just overwhelm her...

Alice and the Devil

'Yes, I can see ghosts,' she said.
'That's why she told me to come here. Because you can help us. You can help grandad and me. You can help us defeat him.'
'Him?'
'Yes, him. The Devil.'

A boy crosses the moors in a storm to plead for Alice's help, claiming to be sent by a ghost.

Is the boy's grandfather really being terrorised by the Devil himself? Alice can't believe it – but then she's experienced things she'd never imagined could come true. But even with her paranormal experiences, little does she expect the horror she is about to face at the lonely rectory overlooking the moors…

Printed in Great Britain
by Amazon